The McKenna Brothers

Three billionaire brothers. Three guarded hearts. Three fabulous stories.

Meet the gorgeous McKenna Brothers…

In this brand-new trilogy from the wonderfully witty, *New York Times* bestselling author Shirley Jump.

Rich, handsome and successful, they're the most eligible bachelors in Boston!

Find out what happens when the oldest brother, Finn, finds himself propositioned by the intriguing, feisty Ellie Winston in

One Day to Find a Husband
July 2012

Discover whether straight-talking Stace Kettering can tame notorious playboy Riley in

How the Playboy Got Serious
August 2012

Returning hero Brody is back home and has a secret…but can he confide in Kate Spencer? Find out in

Return of the Last McKenna
September 2012

Dear Reader,

Writing this book was such fun, because I love Boston (I grew up in the suburbs outside the city) and I love animals. We've been the proud owners of a couple of animal shelter dogs, as well as one stray starving cat that found its way to our porch. Our late Golden Retriever Heidi (who was the best darned dog in the world) is the basis for the Heidi in this book (as well as the basis for the lovable but mischievous Mortise and Tenon in *How to Lasso a Cowboy*). She truly was an amazing dog who has stayed in our hearts long after the day her own heart gave out.

This book introduces the McKenna brothers, starting with the oldest, Finn. I love writing connected books, because it's so much fun to continue a story from one book to the next. You, dear reader, often have a direct impact on that. I'll get a letter or email saying you loved this secondary character, or that one, and want to read more about them. To me, it's like visiting my hometown every time I return to a particular town or family of characters. I guess I'm a bit of a nostalgic person that way—I hold on to old mementos and treasured memories, and love to return home to see friends from way back when.

I love to hear from readers, too, so please write to me through my website (www.shirleyjump.com) or visit my blog (www.shirleyjump.blogspot.com) where I post family favorite recipes and writing advice. And if you have a special pet in your life, share your story, and I'll be sure to include it on my website!

Happy reading,

Shirley

SHIRLEY JUMP

One Day to Find a Husband

TORONTO NEW YORK LONDON
AMSTERDAM PARIS SYDNEY HAMBURG
STOCKHOLM ATHENS TOKYO MILAN MADRID
PRAGUE WARSAW BUDAPEST AUCKLAND

Recycling programs
for this product may
not exist in your area.

ISBN-13: 978-0-373-17821-6

ONE DAY TO FIND A HUSBAND

First North American Publication 2012

www.Harlequin.com

Printed in U.S.A.

New York Times bestselling author **Shirley Jump** didn't have the will-power to diet, nor the talent to master under-eye concealer, so she bowed out of a career in television and opted instead for a career where she could be paid to eat at her desk—writing. At first, seeking revenge on her children for their grocery store tantrums, she sold embarrassing essays about them to anthologies. However, it wasn't enough to feed her growing addiction to writing funny. So she turned to the world of romance novels, where messes are (usually) cleaned up before The End. In the worlds Shirley gets to create and control, the children listen to their parents, the husbands always remember holidays, and the housework is magically done by elves. Though she's thrilled to see her books in stores around the world, Shirley mostly writes because it gives her an excuse to avoid cleaning the toilets and helps feed her shoe habit.

To learn more, visit her website at www.shirleyjump.com.

Books by Shirley Jump

THE PRINCESS TEST
HOW TO LASSO A COWBOY
IF THE RED SLIPPER FITS
VEGAS PREGNANCY SURPRISE
BEST MAN SAYS I DO
A PRINCESS FOR CHRISTMAS
DOORSTEP DADDY
THE BRIDESMAID AND THE BILLIONAIRE
MARRY-ME CHRISTMAS

Other titles by this author available in ebook format.

To my husband, who truly is my hero
every day of my life.

Thank you for blessing me with your love, and
with our amazing children.

CHAPTER ONE

Finn McKenna wanted one thing.

And she was standing fifteen feet away, completely unaware of what he was about to do and definitely not expecting the question he wanted to ask her. He watched the woman—tall, blonde, leggy, the kind any man in his right mind could imagine taking to dinner, twirling around a dance floor, holding close at the end of the night—and hoped like hell his plan worked.

If he was his grandfather, he'd have been toting the McKenna four-leaf clover in his pocket, knocking three times on the banister and whispering a prayer to the Lord above. Finn McKenna's ancestors were nothing if not superstitious. Finn, on the other hand, believed in the kind of luck fostered by good research and hard work. Not the kind brought about by leprechauns and rainbows.

He'd put enough time into this project, that was for sure. Turned the idea left, right and upside down in his head. Done his research, twice over. In short, reassured himself as much as one man could that the lady he was going to talk to would say...

Yes.

"You're insane."

Finn turned and shrugged at his little brother. Riley McKenna had the same dark brown hair and sky-blue eyes as the rest of the McKenna boys, but something about Riley, maybe his grin or his devil-may-care attitude, gave those same features a little spin of dashing. Finn had inherited the serious, hard lines of his workaholic father, where Riley had more of their free-spirited mother's twinkle. "I'm not crazy, Riley. It's business. Risks are part of the job."

"Here." Riley handed him a glass. "I talked the bartender into pouring you and me some good quality Irish ale."

"Thanks." Finn sipped at the dark brew. It slid down his throat with smooth, almost spicy notes. The beer was dry, yet robust, the kind that promised a memorable drink in a single pint. A thick head of foam on top indicated the quality of the ale. Good choice on Riley's part, but Finn wasn't surprised. His little brother knew his brews.

All around him, people mingled and networked over several-hundred-dollar-a-bottle wines and martinis with names so fancy they needed their own dictionary. In this crowd, a beer stuck out like a dandelion in a field of manicured roses, but Finn McKenna had never been one to worry much about breaking the rules or caring what other people thought about him. It was what had fueled his success.

And had also been a part of his recent failure.

A temporary state, he reminded himself. Tonight, he was going to change all of that. He was going to rebuild his business and he was going to use Ellie Winston, interim CEO of WW Architectural Design, to help him do it.

She just didn't know it yet.

Eleanor Winston, known by those close to her as "Ellie," the new boss of WW, her father's company.

Henry Winston Sr., one of the two Ws in the company name, had retired suddenly a couple weeks ago. Rumor was he'd had a major heart attack and would probably not return to the chair. The other W, his brother, had walked out in a family dispute eleven years prior, but his name remained on the masthead.

Finn ticked off what he knew about Eleanor Winston in his head. Twenty-nine, with a master's in design from a reputable college, three years working at a firm in Atlanta before moving to Boston shortly after her father's illness. Her design work was primarily in residential housing—the McMansions much maligned by the architectural world—and Finn had heard she was none too pleased to be spending her days designing hospitals and office supertowers. All the more reason for her to accept his offer with gratitude. He'd scoped out his competition for several weeks before deciding WW Architects was the best choice. A fledgling president, overseeing a sprawling company with multiple projects going at any given time—surely she wanted a...helping hand. Yes, that's what he'd call it. A helping hand. A win-win for her and him.

"So this is your grand plan? Talking to Ellie Winston? Here? Now?" Riley asked. "With you dressed like that?"

Finn glanced down at his dark gray pinstripe suit, crisp white shirt and navy blue tie. "What's wrong with the way I'm dressed?"

"Hey, nothing, if you're heading to a funeral." Riley patted his own shirt, as usual unbuttoned at the neck and devoid of a tie. "Make a statement, Finn. Get your sexy on."

Finn shook off that advice. Riley was the more colorful McKenna brother, the one who always stood out in a crowd. Finn preferred his appearance neat, trim and professional—the same way he conducted business. Nothing too flashy, nothing too exciting.

"This is the perfect environment," Finn said, nodding toward the woman. "She's relaxed, maybe had a couple glasses of wine, and best of all—" he turned to his brother "—not expecting the offer I'm about to make."

Riley chuckled. "Oh, I think that's guaranteed."

Finn's gaze centered on Ellie Winston again. She laughed at something the guy beside her said. A full-throated laugh, her head thrown back, her deep green eyes dancing with merriment. Every time he'd seen her, she'd been like that—so open, so exuberant. Something dark and deep stirred in Finn's gut, and for a split second he envied the man at her side. Wondered what it would be like to be caught in that spell. To be the one making her laugh and smile like that.

Damn, she was beautiful. Intriguing.

And a distraction, he told himself. One he couldn't afford. Hadn't he already learned that lesson from one painful mistake after another?

"A woman like that…" Riley shook his head. "I don't think hardball is the right way to play it, Hawk."

"I hate when you call me that."

"Hey, if the nickname fits." Riley grinned. "You, big brother, spy the weak, pluck them up and use them to feather your nest." He put a hand on Finn's shoulder. "But in the nicest way possible. Of course."

"Oh, yeah, of course." A magazine had dubbed Finn "the Hawk" a few years ago when he'd done a surprise buyout of his closest competitor. Then six months later, his next closest competitor. He'd absorbed the other businesses into his own, becoming one of the largest architectural firms in New England. At least for a while. Until his ex-girlfriend's betrayal had reduced his company to half its size, taking his reputation down at the same time.

Now he'd slipped in the rankings, not even powerful enough to make any lists anymore. Or to merit any other nickname other than "Failure."

But not for long.

A waitress came by with a tray of crudités and offered some to Finn and Riley. Finn waved off the food, but Riley picked up a smoked salmon–topped cucumber slice and shot the waitress a grin. "Are these as delicious as you are beautiful?"

A flush filled her face and she smiled. "You'll have to try one to see."

He popped it in his mouth, chewed and swallowed. Then shot her an even bigger grin. "The appetizer is definitely a winner."

The waitress cocked her hip and gave him another, sassier smile. "Perhaps you should try the other, too." Then she turned on her heel and headed for the next group.

"Perhaps I will," Riley said, watching her sashay through the crowd.

Finn rolled his eyes. Keeping Riley focused on the subject at hand sometimes required superhuman abilities. "Do you ever think about anything other than women?"

"Do you ever think about anything other than business?" Riley countered.

"I'm the owner, Riley. I don't have a choice but to keep my eye on the ball and my focus on the company." He'd had a time where he'd focused on a relationship— and that had cost him dearly. Never again.

"There's always a choice, Finn." Riley grinned. "I prefer the ones that end with a woman like that in my bed, and a smile on my face." He arched a brow in the direction of the waitress, who shot him a flirtatious smile back. "A woman like that one."

"You're a dog."

Riley shrugged off the teasing. His playboy tendencies had been well documented by the Boston media. As the youngest McKenna, getting away with murder had been his middle name almost since birth. Funny how stereotypical the three boys had turned out. Finn, the eldest, the responsible one, working since he was thirteen. Brody, the middle brother, the peacemaker, who worked a respectable, steady job as a family physician. And then Riley, the youngest, and thus overindulged by their mother, and later, by their grandmother, who still doted on the "baby" of the family. Riley had turned being a wild child into a sport…and managed to live a life almost entirely devoid of responsibility.

Finn sometimes felt like he'd been responsible from the day he took his first steps. He'd started out as a one-man shop right out of college, and built McKenna Designs into a multioffice corporation designing projects all over the world. His rapid growth, coupled with a recession that fell like an axe on the building industry, and one mistake he wished he could go back in time and undo, had damaged his bottom line. Nearly taken him to bankruptcy.

"Carpe diem, Finn," Riley said. "You should try it sometime. Get out of the office and live a little."

"I do."

Riley laughed. Out loud. *"Right."*

"Running a company is a demanding job," Finn said. Across the room, the woman he wanted to talk to was still making small talk with the other partygoers. To Finn, the room seemed like an endless sea of blue and black, neckties and polished loafers. Only two people stood out in the dark ocean before him—

Riley, who had bucked the trend by wearing a collarless white shirt under a sportscoat trimmed to fit his physique.

And Eleanor Winston, who'd opted for a deep cranberry dress that wrapped around her slender frame, emphasizing her small waist, and hourglass shape. She was the only woman in a colorful dress, the only one who looked like she was truly at a cocktail party, not a funeral, as Riley would say. She had on high heels in a light neutral color, making her legs seem impossibly long. They curved in tight calf muscles, leading up to creamy thighs and—

Concentrate.

He had a job to do and getting distracted would only cost him in the end.

"You seem to make it harder than most, though. For Pete's sake, you have a sofa bed in your office." Riley chuckled and shook his head. "If that doesn't scream lonely bachelor with no life, I don't know what does. Unless Miss Marstein is keeping you warm at night."

Finn choked on the sip of beer in his mouth. His assistant was an efficient, persnickety woman in her early sixties who ran his office and schedule with an iron fist. "Miss Marstein is old enough to be my grandmother."

"And you're celibate enough to be a monk. Get away from the blueprints, Hawk, and live a little."

Finn let out a sigh. Riley didn't get it. He'd always been the younger, irresponsible one, content to live off the inheritance from their parents' death, rather than carry the worries of a job. Riley didn't understand the precarious position McKenna Designs was in right now. How one mistake could cost him all the ground he'd regained, one painful step at a time. People were depending on Finn to succeed. His employees had families, mortgages, car payments. He couldn't let them down. It was about far greater things than Finn's reputation or bottom line.

Finn bristled. "I work long days and yes, sometimes nights. It's more efficient to have a sofa bed—"

"Efficient? Try depressing." Riley tipped his beer toward the woman across from them. "If you were smart, you'd think about getting wild with *her* on that sofa bed. Sleep's overrated. While sex, on the other hand…" He grinned. "Can't rate it highly enough."

"I do not have time for something like that. The company has been damaged by this roller-coaster economy and…" He shook his head. Regret weighed down his shoulders. "I never should have trusted her."

Riley placed a hand on Finn's shoulder. "Stop beating yourself up. Everyone makes mistakes."

"Still, I never should have trusted her," he said again. How many times had he said that to himself? A hundred times? Two hundred? He could say it a thousand and it wouldn't undo the mistake.

"You were in love. All men act like idiots when they're in love." Riley grinned. "Take it from the expert."

"You've been in love? Real, honest-to-goodness love?"

Riley shrugged. "It felt real at the time."

"Well, I won't make that mistake again." Finn took a deep gulp of beer.

"You're hopeless. One bad relationship is no reason to become a hermit."

One bad relationship? Finn had fallen for a woman who had stolen his top clients, smeared his reputation and broken his heart. That wasn't a bad relationship, it was the sinking of the Titanic. He'd watched his parents

struggle through a terrible marriage, both of them un-
happily mismatched, and didn't want to make the same
mistake.

"I'm not having this conversation right now." Finn's
gaze went to Ellie Winston again. She had moved on to
another group of colleagues. She greeted nearly everyone she saw, with a smile, a few words, a light touch.
And they responded in kind. She had socializing down to
an art. The North Carolina transplant had made friends
quickly. Only a few weeks in the city and she was winning over the crowd of their peers with one hand tied
behind her back. Yes, she'd be an asset to his company
and his plan. A good one. "I'm focused on work."

"Seems to me you're focused on her." Riley grinned.

"She's a means to an end, nothing more."

"Yeah, well, the only ending I see for you, Finn, is
one where you're old and gray, surrounded by paperwork
and sleeping alone in that sofa bed."

"You're wrong."

For a while, Finn had thought he could have both the
life and the job. He'd even bought the ring, put a down-
payment on a house in the suburbs. He'd lost his head
for a while, a naive young man who believed love could
conquer everything. Until that love had stabbed him in
the back.

Apparently true love was a fairy tale reserved for others. Like kissing the Blarney Stone for good luck.

Finn now preferred to have his relationships as dry
as his wine. No surprises, no twists and turns. Just a
dependable, predictable sameness. Leaving the roller
coaster for the corporate world.

He suspected, though, that Eleanor Winston and her
standout maroon dress was far from the dry, dependable
type. She had a glint in her eye, a devilish twinkle in

her smile, a spontaneous air about her that said getting involved with her would leave a man…

Breathless.

Exactly the opposite of what he wanted. He would have to keep a clear head around her.

Ellie drifted away from her companions, heading toward the door. Weaving through the crowd slowed her progress, but it wouldn't be long before she'd finished her goodbyes and left. "She's leaving. Catch up with you later," he said to Riley.

"Take a page from my book, brother, and simply ask her out for a drink," Riley said, then as Finn walked away, added one more bit of advice. "And for God's sake, Finn, don't talk business. At least not until…after." He grinned. "And if you get stumped, think to yourself, 'What would Riley say?' That'll work, I promise."

Finn waved off Riley's advice. Riley's attention had already strayed back to the waitress, who was making her way through the room with another tray—and straight for Riley's charming grin. His brother's eyes were always focused on the next beautiful woman he could take home to his Back Bay townhouse. Finn had much bigger, and more important goals.

Like saving his company. He'd made millions already in architecture, and hopefully would again, if he could make his business profitable again. If not, he could always accept his grandmother's offer and take up the helm at McKenna Media. The family business, started a generation ago by his grandfather, who used to go door-to-door selling radio ad space to local businesses. Finn's father had joined the company after high school and taken it into television, before his death when Finn was eleven. Ever since his grandfather had died three years ago, Finn's grandmother had sat in the top chair, but she'd been making noise lately about wanting to retire and have Finn take over, and keep the company in McKenna hands. Finn's heart, though, lay in architecture. Tonight was all about keeping that heartbeat going.

Finn laid his still-full glass of beer on the tray of a passing waiter, then straightened his tie and worked a smile to his face. Riley, who never tired of telling Finn he was too uptight, too stiff, would say it was more of a grimace. Finn didn't care. He wasn't looking to be a cover model or to make friends.

Then he glanced over at his brother—no longer chatting up the waitress but now flirting with a brunette. For a second, Finn envied Riley's easy way with women. Everything about his little brother screamed relaxed, at home. His stance, his smile, the slight rumple in his shirt.

Finn forced himself to relax, to look somewhat approachable. Then he increased his pace to close the gap between himself and Ellie. He reached her just before she stepped through the glass doors of the lobby.

"Miss Winston."

She stopped, her hand on the metal bar, ready to exit. Then she turned back and faced him. Her long blond hair swung with the movement, settling like a silk curtain around her shoulders. The short-sleeved crimson dress she wore hugged her curves, and dropped into a tantalizing yet modest V at her chest. For a second, her green eyes were blank, then she registered his face and the green went from cold emerald to warm forest. "My goodness. Mr. McKenna," she said. "I recognize you from the article in *Architecture Today*."

"Please, call me Finn." She'd seen the piece about his award for innovative building design? And remembered it? "That was more than a year ago. I'm impressed with your memory."

"Well, like most people in our industry, I have an absolutely ridiculous attention for detail." She smiled then, the kind of smile that no one would ever confuse with a grimace. The kind of smile that hit a man in the gut and made him forget everything around him. The kind of smile that added an extra sparkle to her green eyes, and lit her delicate features with an inner glow.

Intoxicating.

Get a grip, McKenna. This was business, nothing more. Since when did he think of anything other than a bottle of single malt as intoxicating? Business, and business *only.* "If you have a minute, I wanted to talk to you."

"Actually I'm heading out." She gestured toward the door. A continual Morse code of headlights went by on the busy street outside, tires making a constant whoosh-whoosh of music on the dark pavement, even though it was nearing midnight on a Tuesday night. Boston, like most cities, never slept. And neither, most nights, did Finn McKenna.

"Perhaps you could call my assistant," she said, "and set up a meeting for—"

"If you have time tonight, I would appreciate it." He remembered Riley's advice and decided to sweeten the pot a little. Show her he wasn't the cold business-only gargoyle that people rumored him to be. Hawk indeed. Finn could be suave. Debonair even.

His younger brother could charm a free coffee from a barista; talk a traffic cop into forgetting his ticket. Maybe if Finn applied a bit of that, it might loosen her up, and make her more amenable to what he was about to propose. So he worked up another smile-grimace to his face—and tried another tack.

"Why don't we, uh, grab a couple drinks somewhere?" he said, then groaned inwardly. Casual conversation was clearly not his forte. Put him in a board room, and he was fine, but attempting small talk…a disaster.

Damn Riley's advice anyway.

"Thank you, but I don't drink. If you ask me, too many bad decisions have been made with a bottle of wine." Another smile. "I'm sure if you call in the morning—"

"Your schedule is certainly as busy as mine. Why don't we avoid yet another meeting?"

"In other words, get this out of the way and then I can get rid of you?"

He laughed. "Something like that."

"It's really late…"

He could see her hesitation. In a second, she'd say no again, and he'd be forced to delay his plan one more day. He didn't have the luxury of time. He needed to get a meeting with Ellie Winston—a private one—now. In business, he knew when to press, and when to step back. Now was a time to press. A little. "I promise, I don't bite."

"Or pick over the remains of your competitors?"

"That's a rumor. Nothing more. I've only done that… once." He paused a second. "Okay, maybe twice."

She threw back her head and laughed. "Oh my, Mr. McKenna. You are not what I expected."

What had she expected? That he would be the stern predator portrayed in that article? Or that he wouldn't have a sense of humor? "I hope that's a good thing."

"We shall see," she said. Then she reached out and laid a hand on his arm, a quick touch, nothing more, but it was enough to stir a fire inside him. A fire that he knew better than to stoke.

What the hell had been in that beer? Finn McKenna wasn't a man given to spontaneous emotional or physical reactions. Except for one brief window, he'd lived his life as ordered as the buildings he designed. No room for fluff or silliness. And particularly no room for the foolishness of a tumble in the hay. Yet his mind considered that very thing when Eleanor Winston touched him.

"I'm sorry, you're absolutely right, it is late and you must want to get home," he said, taking a step back, feeling…flustered, which was not at all like him. "I'll call your assistant in the morning."

Riley had said to say what he would say. And Finn knew damned well Riley wouldn't have said that.

"No, I'm the one who's sorry, Mr. McKenna. I've had a long, long day and I…" She glanced back in the direction of the closed double doors, but Finn got the sense she wasn't looking at the black-tie crowd filling the Park Plaza's ballroom, but at something else, something he couldn't see. Then she glanced at her watch. "Midnight. Well, the day *is* over, isn't it?"

"If you want it to be, Cinderella. Or you could continue the ball for a little while longer." The quip came out without hesitation. A true Riley-ism. He'd been spending too much time with his brother.

Or maybe not, he thought, when she laughed. He liked her laugh. It was light, airy, almost musical.

"Cinderella, huh?" she said. "Okay, you convinced me. It would be nice to end my day with some one-on-one conversation instead of an endless stream of small talk." She wagged a finger at him and a tease lit her face, made her smile quirk higher on one side than the other. "But I'll have tea, not tequila, while I hear you out on whatever it is you want to tell me."

"Excellent." He could only hope she was as amenable to his proposal. Surely such an auspicious beginning boded well for the rest. He pushed on the door and waved Ellie through with one long sweep of his arm. "After you...Cinderella."

"My goodness, Finn McKenna. You certainly do know how to make a girl swoon." She flashed him yet another smile and then whooshed past him and out into the night, leaving the faint scent of jasmine and vanilla in her wake.

Get back to the plan, he reminded himself. Focus on getting her to agree. Nothing more. He could do it, he knew he could. Finn wasn't a distracted, spontaneous man. He refused to tangle personal with business ever again. He would get Ellie to agree, and before he could blink, his company would be back on top.

But as he followed one of his biggest competitors into the twinkling, magical world of Boston at night, he had to wonder if he was making the best business decision of his life—or the worst.

CHAPTER TWO

SHE had to be crazy.

What else had made Ellie agree to midnight drinks with Finn McKenna—one of her competitors and a man she barely knew? She'd been ready to go home, get to bed and get some much-needed sleep when Finn had approached her.

There'd been something about his smile, though, something about him charmed her. He wasn't a smooth talker, more a man who had an easy, approachable way about him, one that she suspected rarely showed in his business life. The "Hawk" moniker that magazine—and most of the people in the architecture world—had given him didn't fit the man who had teasingly called her Cinderella. A man with vivid sky-blue eyes and dark chocolate hair.

And that intrigued her. A lot.

So Ellie settled into the red vinyl covered seat across from Finn McKenna, a steaming mug of tea warming her palms. So far they'd done little more than exchange small talk about the weather and the party they'd just left.

She'd never met the fabled architect, the kind of man talked about in hushed tones by others in the industry. She'd read about him, even studied a few of his projects when she was in college, but they'd never crossed paths.

If she hadn't been at the helm of WW Architectural Design, she wouldn't even have been at the event tonight, one of those networking things designed to bring together competitors, as if they'd share trade secrets over a few glasses of wine. In reality, everyone was there to try to extract as much information as they could, while revealing none of their own.

"Was that your brother you were talking to in the ballroom?" she asked. Telling herself she wasn't being curious about the contradictory Finn, just conversational.

Finn nodded. "Riley. He's the youngest."

"He looks a lot like you."

Finn chuckled. "Poor guy."

"Is he in the industry, too?"

"Definitely not. He tagged along for the free drinks."

She laughed. "I can appreciate that. Either way, I'm glad that cocktail party is over." She rubbed her neck, loosening some of the tension of the day. "Sometimes it seems those things are never going to end."

"You seemed to fit right in."

"I can talk, believe me." She laughed, then leaned in closer and lowered her voice to a conspiratorial whisper. "But in reality, I hate those kinds of events."

"You and me both. Everyone trying to pretend to be nice, when really they just want to find out what you're up to and how they can steal that business away from you," Finn said. "I think of them as a necessary evil."

She laughed again. "We definitely have that in common." She'd never expected to have anything in common with Finn McKenna, whose reputation had painted him as a ruthless competitor, exactly her opposite. Or to find him attractive. But she did.

"I don't know about you, but I'm much happier behind my desk, sketching out a design. Anything is better than trading the same chatter with the same people in an endless social circle."

"You and I could be twins. I feel exactly the same way. But…" She let out a sigh and spun her teacup gently left and right.

"But what?"

"But I stepped into my father's shoes, and that means doing things as he did." People expected the head of WW to be involved, interactive and most of all, friendly, so Ellie had gone to the event and handled it, she hoped, as her father would have. She had thought taking over her father's position would be a temporary move, but after the news the doctor gave her yesterday…

Ellie bit back a sigh. There were many, many dinners like that in her future. Henry Winston's heart attack had been a bad one, leaving him with greatly diminished cardiac capacity. The doctor had warned her that too much stress and worry could be fatal. A return to work was a distant possibility right now. If ever. It all depended on his recovery. Either way, Ellie was determined to keep WW running, and not worry her father with any of the details. He came first.

"Have you ever met my father?" she asked Finn.

He nodded. "I have. Nice guy. Straight shooter."

"And a talker. I inherited that from him." Ellie smiled, thinking of the father she'd spent so many hours with in the last few years, chatting about design and business and life. Her father had worked constantly when Ellie was young and been gone too much for them to build any kind of relationship. But ever since Ellie went to college, Henry had made a more concerted effort to connect with his daughter. Although she loved her mother dearly, Ellie wasn't as close to Marguerite, who had moved to California shortly after divorcing Henry when Ellie was eighteen. "My father likes to say that he never knows where his next opportunity might come from, so he greets the cashier at a fast food place as heartily as he does the owner of a bank."

"People like that about him. Your father is well respected."

"Thank you." The compliment warmed Ellie. "I hope I can live up to his example."

"I'm sure you will."

The conversation stalled between them. Finn turned his attention to his coffee, but didn't drink, just held the mug. Ellie nursed her tea, then added more sugar to the slightly bitter brew.

She watched Finn, wondering why he had invited her out. If he wanted to talk business, he was taking his time getting to it. What other reason could he have? For all the joking between them earlier, she had a feeling he wasn't here for a date.

Finn McKenna was younger than she'd expected. Surely a man with his reputation had to be ten feet tall, and ten years older than the early thirties she guessed him to be? Heck, he seemed hardly older than her, but his resume stretched a mile longer. What surprised her most was that he had sought her out—her—out of all the other people in that room. Why?

He had opted for coffee, black, but didn't drink from the cup. He crossed his hands on the table before him, in precise, measured moments. He held himself straight— uptight, she would have called it—and kept his features as unreadable as a blank sheet of paper. He wasn't cold, exactly, more…

Impassive. Like the concrete used to construct his buildings. The teasing man she'd met in the lobby had been replaced by someone far more serious. Had that Finn been a fluke? Which was the real Finn McKenna?

And more, why did she care so much?

"I heard WW got the contract on the Piedmont hospital project," he said.

"We haven't even announced that hospital deal yet," she replied, halting her tea halfway to her lips. "How did you know about it?"

"It's my business to know." He smiled. "Congratulations."

"Thank you." She wanted to tell him the thought of such a big project daunted her, particularly without her father's valuable advice. She wanted to tell Finn that she worried the hospital design would be too big, too detailed for her to oversee successfully, and most of all, she wanted to ask him how he had done it for so long single-handedly, but she didn't.

She already knew the answer. She'd read it in the interview in *Architect* magazine. Finn McKenna wasted little time. He had no hobbies, he told the reporter, and organized his workdays in the most efficient way possible, in order to cram twenty hours of work into twelve.

And, she knew better than to trust him. He hadn't earned the nickname Hawk by being nice to his competitors. No matter how they sliced this, she was one of his competitors and needed to be on her guard. For all she knew, Finn was working right this second—and working an angle with her that would benefit his business.

At that moment, as if making her thoughts a reality, Finn's cell phone rang. He let out a sigh, then shot her an apologetic smile. "Sorry. I have to take this. It's a client who's in California right now, while we build his new offices here. I think he forgot about the time change. This should only take a second."

"No problem. I understand." She watched him deal with the call and realized that Finn McKenna had made himself a success by sacrificing a life. That wasn't what Ellie had wanted when she had gone into architectural design, but the more time she spent behind her father's desk, the more it became clear that was where she was heading.

That was the one thing her father didn't want to see. She thought back to the conversation they'd had this morning. *Don't end up like me, Ellie Girl. Get married. Settle down. Have a life instead of just a business, and don't neglect your family to protect the bottom line. Do it before...*

He hadn't had to finish the sentence. She knew the unspoken words—before he was gone. The heart attack had set off a ticking clock inside Henry and nearly every visit he encouraged Ellie to stop putting her life on hold.

The trouble was, she had quickly found that running WW Architectural Design and having a life were mutually exclusive. Now things were more complicated, her time more precious. And having it all seemed to be an impossible idea.

She thought of the picture in her purse, the dozens more on her phone, and the paperwork waiting on her desk. Waiting not for her signature, but for a miracle. One that would keep the promise she had made in China last year.

Nearly three years ago, Ellie had been on the fast track at an architectural firm in North Carolina. Then she'd gone to a conference in China, gotten lost on the way to the hotel and ended up meeting a woman who changed her life.

Ellie never made it to the hotel or the conference. She spent five days helping Sun Yuchin dig a well and repair a neighbor's house in a tiny, cramped town, and fallen in love with the simple village, and bonded with the woman who lived there. Every few months since, Ellie had returned. She'd been there to meet Sun's daughter, Jiao, after she was born, even helped feed the baby, and the following year, helped build an extra room for the child. In the process, Ellie had formed a deep friendship with Sun, a hardworking, single mother who had suffered more tragedies than any person should in a lifetime—her parents dead, then her husband two years later, and near the end of one of Ellie's trips to Sun's town, the woman finally confided the worst news of all.

Sun had cancer. Stage four. After she told Ellie, she asked her an incredible question.

Will you raise Jiao after I'm gone? Take her to America, and be her mother?

Finn ended the call, then put his cell back into his pocket. "The Piedmont hospital will be quite an undertaking for WW," he said, drawing her attention back to the topic.

Was he curious, or jealous? His firm had been one of the few invited to submit a bid. She remembered her father being so sure that McKenna Designs, clearly the leader in experience, would land the job. But in the end, either her father's schmoozing on the golf course or his more competitive bid had won out and McKenna Designs had been left in the dust.

Was this true congratulations or sour grapes?

Ellie gave Finn a nod, then crossed her hands on the table. "I'm sure we're up to the challenge." Did her voice betray the doubts she felt?

"I know a project of that size can seem intimidating," he added, as if he'd read her mind. "Even for someone with your experience."

The dig didn't go unnoticed. She was sure a methodical man like Finn McKenna would already know she'd built her career in residential, not commercial properties. He was expressing his doubts in her ability without coming right out and saying it.

He wasn't the only one with concerns. She'd gone into architecture because she loved the field, and chosen residential work because she loved creating that happy home for her clients, and had been rewarded well for that job. She'd never wanted to be a part of the more impersonal, commercial industry.

But now she was. And that meant she had to deal with everything that came her way, no matter what. And handle it, one way or another, because her father's company needed her to. She couldn't go to her father and risk raising his blood pressure. She'd muddle through this project on her own. No matter what, Ellie would hold on to what Henry had built.

"We have a strong, dedicated team," she said.

"Had."

"Excuse me?"

"You *had* a strong, dedicated team. As I hear it, Farnsworth quit last week."

Damn. Finn really did have his finger on the pulse of WW Architectural Design. Few people knew George Farnsworth, one of the oldest and most experienced architects at the firm, had quit. He'd butted heads with Ellie almost from the day she walked in the door, and eventually said he'd work for her father—or no one at all. Which wasn't quite true, because it turned out Farnsworth had had a lucrative job offer at a competitor waiting in the wings the whole time.

She'd been scrambling ever since to find a worthy replacement. And coming up empty.

"You seem to know quite a bit about my business, Mr. McKenna—"

"Finn, please."

"Finn, then." She pushed the cup of tea to the side and leaned forward. "What I want to know is why."

He gave her a half-nod. "What they say about you is true."

"And what, pray tell, do they say about me?"

"That you're smart and capable. And able to talk your way out of or into just about anything."

She laughed. "The talking part is probably true. My father always said I could talk my way out of a concrete box."

"Refill?" The waitress hovered over their table, coffeepot halfway to Finn's cup. Then she noticed the two still-full cups. "Okay, guess not."

Finn paused long enough for the waitress to leave, then his sky-blue gaze zeroed in on hers. "You asked why I have such an interest in your business, and in you."

She nodded.

"I've done my research on your career, Miss Winston, and on WW Architectural Design because—" he paused a beat "—I have a proposition for you."

"A proposition?" Ellie arched a brow, then flipped on the charm. Two could dance in this conversation. Finn McKenna had yet to tell her anything of substance, and she refused to give away her surprise or her curiosity. He had likely underestimated her as a businesswoman, and after tonight, she doubted he'd do it again. "Why, Finn, that sounds positively scandalous."

He let out a short, dry laugh. "I assure you, Miss Winston—"

"Ellie." She gave him a nod and a slight smile. She had found that a little warmth and charm, accented by the slight Southern accent that she'd picked up in her years in North Carolina, often served her well in business dealings, and she used that tool to her advantage now. No giving Finn McKenna the upperhand. No, she wanted to know what he was after, and more importantly, why. "That's the least you can do, considering I'm calling you by your first name."

"Ellie, then." Her name rolled off his tongue, smooth as caramel. "I…I can assure you—" he paused a second again, seemed to gather his thoughts "—that my proposition is business only."

She waited for him to continue, while her tea cooled in front of her. This was the reason he'd asked her here—not for a date, but for business. A flicker of disappointment ran through her, but she told herself it was for the best. Despite what her father had asked of her, she didn't see how she could possibly fit dating, much less marriage, into her already busy life.

She had her father to worry about and care for, a company to run, and most of all, a home to prepare for the changes coming her way very soon. Getting involved with Finn McKenna didn't even make it on to that list. Heck, it wasn't even in the same galaxy as her other priorities.

"I know that without Farnsworth, you're in a difficult position," Finn continued. "He's the most senior architect on your staff, and you're about to undertake a major hospital project. The kind of thing WW has built its reputation on, and the kind of job that will bring millions into the company coffers."

She nodded. The Piedmont hospital was a huge boon for WW. Her father had worked long and hard to land that project. He was proud as punch to add it on to the company resume, and she was determined not to let her father down. This job would also firmly establish WW's place as a leader in medical facility design—a smart move in an era of increased demand from aging baby boomers.

"As the new CEO," Finn went on in the same precise, no-nonsense manner as before, "you're already at a vulnerable juncture, and losing this project, or screwing it up, could cause WW irreparable damage." He'd clearly studied her, and the company, and was offering an honest, if not a bit too true, perspective. He squared his spoon beside his cup, seeming to gather his thoughts, but she got the feeling he was inserting a measured, calculated pause.

She waited him out. A part of her was glad he'd gotten right to the point, avoiding the male-female flirting dance. She'd met far too many businessmen who thought they could finesse their way through a deal with a few compliments and smiles. Men who saw a woman in charge and took her to be an idiot, or someone they could manipulate over dinner. Finn McKenna, she suspected, was a what-you-see-is-what-you-get man, who saw no need for frills or extra words. Straightforward, to the point, no games. That brief moment in the lobby had been a fluke, she decided. This was the real Finn, aka the Hawk. He wanted something from her and clearly intended to stay until he had it.

"I have two senior architects on my staff who are more than capable of handling the hospital project for you," Finn said. "If you agree to this business proposition, then they would oversee it, sort of as architects on loan. You, Miss Winston—" he paused again, corrected himself "—Ellie, would remain in complete control. And myself and my staff at McKenna Designs would be there as a resource for you, as you navigate the complicated arena of medical facility design, and the troubled waters of the CEO world."

Troubled waters? Did he think she was totally incompetent? She tamped down the rush of anger and feigned flattery.

"That's a mighty nice offer, Finn. Why, a girl would be all aflutter from your generosity..." Then she dropped the Southern Belle accent from her voice, and the smile from her face. He'd made it all sound so smooth, as if the benefit was all to her, not to him. "*If* she hadn't been raised by a father who told her that no one does anything without a payoff. So, I ask you—" she leaned in, her gaze locking on his "—what's in this for you?"

He gave her a short nod, a brief smile, a look that said touché. And something that looked a lot like respect. "My business has struggled as of late. Partly the economy, partly—" the next words seemed to leave his mouth with a sour taste "—because of a project that had some unfortunate results. Although we have a few medical buildings on our resume, our work has primarily been in the retail and corporate world. McKenna Designs would like to move into the medical building field because it's a growing industry that dovetails well with our other corporate work. You would like to strengthen your position as the new head at WW by designing a hospital that puts a really big star in the company constellation, as they say." He spread his hands. "A partnership benefits us both."

"From what *I've* heard, McKenna Designs took a serious blow in credibility and finances over this past year and you've been reeling ever since." They worked in a small industry and people talked. The people who worked for Ellie had been more than happy to fill her in on the local competition when she arrived in Boston. Finn McKenna's name had come up several times.

"We've had our…challenges."

"As have we," she acknowledged.

"Precisely the reason I came to you." Now he leaned back and sipped at his coffee, even though it had surely gone cold long ago. He was waiting for her to make the next move.

As she looked at him, she realized two things. He didn't think she was capable of running the firm without his help and two, he was offering a deal that benefited him far more than her. She could hire another architect— maybe even, with the right incentives, steal Finn's best and brightest right from under his nose—and be just fine. He was just like all the other men she had met, and all the "concerned" colleagues of her father, who saw the little Winston girl as nothing more than a figurehead.

The Hawk was merely swooping in to try to scoop up an opportunity. This meeting had been a waste of time. The one luxury Ellie Winston didn't have.

She rose, grabbing her purse as she did. "I appreciate the offer, I really do, but we're just fine at WW, and we'll be just fine without an alliance with you. So thank you again—" she fished in her purse for a few dollars, and tossed them on the table "—but I must decline. Good evening, Mr. McKenna."

Then she left, hoping that was the last she saw of Finn McKenna.

CHAPTER THREE

ELLIE had vowed not to think about Finn's surprise offer. He was only out for number one, she had decided last night during the cab ride home, and she'd be a fool to even consider it. But as the morning's staff meeting progressed, she found her mind wandering back to that diner conversation.

You're at a vulnerable juncture.

Losing this project could mean irreparable damage.

A partnership benefits us both.

Had he meant what he said? Could it be a genuine offer? And if she accepted, would the benefits outweigh the drawbacks? Or was he trying to get in—and then take over her company? She'd heard how many times he'd done that to other firms.

She had floated Finn's name with a few of her colleagues this morning, trying to get more of a read on the man everyone dubbed "the Hawk." To a person, they'd urged caution, reminding her Finn "preferred to eat the competition for lunch rather than lunch with them."

That meant any sort of alliance with him required serious consideration. Was his proposal all a way for him to take over her father's company? Or would his proposal be a true two-way benefit?

She thought of what lay ahead for her life, about the

child about to become a part of her life, and wondered how she could possibly juggle it all. Was a partnership a good idea?

"I'm worried, Ellie." Larry, the most senior of her remaining architects let out a long breath. "We really need a strong leader on this project. Even though we have a lot of great architects here, without either your dad or Farnsworth to head this, well…"

"We don't have anyone with enough experience and that means we'll be in over our head from day one," Ellie finished for him. She'd known that going in, but had hoped that when she called the staff meeting someone would step up to the plate and produce a resume rife with medical design experience. Hadn't happened. "We have a great team here, I agree. But no one who has direct experience with medical institutions."

Larry nodded. "If we were building a bank, a resort, a hotel, we'd be fine. We could do those in our sleep. And I'm sure we could handle this project, too, but we'd be a whole lot better off with a good senior architect to oversee all those details. As it is, we're stretched thin with the new mall out on Route 1 and the condo project in the Back Bay."

Ellie knew Larry made sense. Between the integrated technology, clean environment requirements and strict government guidelines, a hospital build was so much more complex than an ordinary office building. Farnsworth's specialty had been in that arena, and without him, the team would be on a constant scramble to check regs, meet with contractors and double check every element. "I'll find someone."

"By the end of the week?" Panic raised the pitch in Larry's voice. "Because the initial drawings are due by the fifteenth."

Just a few short days away. "Did Farnsworth get anything done on them?"

Larry shook his head. Ellie's gut clenched. Farnsworth had lied and told her he'd done the initial work, but clearly his disgruntled attitude had been affecting his work for a while. Her father had designed several hospitals and medical buildings over the years, but Ellie certainly couldn't go to him for help, and no one on the current staff at WW had the kind of experience her father and Farnsworth had. She'd just have to hire someone.

But by the end of this week? Someone who could step right in and take the project's reins without a single misstep? And then produce a plan that would meet the critical eye of the hospital owners? She needed someone with years of experience. Someone smart. Someone capable, organized. And ready to become the team leader at a moment's notice.

"I'll find someone," she repeated again. "By the end of the day. I promise."

Ellie gave her team a smile, and waited until everyone had left the room before she let the stress and worry consume her. She doodled across the pad in front of her. It was a good thirty seconds before she realized she hadn't sketched a flower or a box or a stick figure. She'd written a name.

And maybe…an answer. The only problem was right now, this was more of a win for Finn, who would reap the benefits of a partnership, the prestige of the project and a cut of the profits, than for Ellie, who risked looking like a company that couldn't do the job and had to call in outsiders.

She tapped her pencil on the pad. There had to be something Finn could give her that would make a part-

nership worth the risk of an alliance with the predatory
Hawk. It would have to be something big, she mused.

Very big.

Finn sat at his massive mahogany desk, the same one he
had bought ten years ago at a garage sale, refinished by
hand then installed on his first day at McKenna Designs.
Back then, he'd had an office not much bigger than the
desk, but as he'd moved up, the desk had moved with
him. Now it sat in the center of his office, his headquar-
ters for watching the world go by eleven stories below
him. Friday morning had dawned bright and beautiful,
with a spring sun determined to coax the flowers from
their leaf cocoons. It was the kind of spring day that
tempted people to call in sick and spend the day by the
Charles River, picnicking and boating and jogging on
the Esplanade. The kind of day that drew everyone out
of their winter huddles, spilling into the parks and onto
the sidewalks, like newly released prisoners.

But not Finn. He had called an early meeting this
morning, and had been snowed under with work every
second since then. Sometimes he felt like he was just
plugging holes in a leaky water bucket. They'd lost another client today, a corporation that said they'd "lost
confidence" in McKenna Designs after hearing of the
defection of two other major clients. Apparently Lucy's
betrayal was still hitting his bottom line, even more than
a year later. He sighed.

He'd turn this company around, one way or another.
He'd hoped that Ellie Winston would hear his offer and
jump at the opportunity for some help. She was out of
her league on the Piedmont project, and definitely didn't
have anyone on her staff who could handle something

of that magnitude. When he'd considered his offer, he'd seen it only as a win-win for her. Yet still she'd said no.

It was a rare defeat to a man who had won nearly everything he put his mind to. The refusal had left him surprised, but not for long. He would regroup, and find another way to convince Ellie that his proposal was in her best interests.

Could she be thinking of hiring someone else? He hadn't heard rumors of anyone considering a job at WW, but that didn't mean there wasn't a prospective candidate. Finn had always prided himself on having an ear to the ground in Boston's busy and competitive architecture world, but that didn't mean he knew everything.

"Knock, knock. Time for lunch."

Finn glanced up and saw his brother standing in the doorway, grinning like a fool. Every time he saw Riley, his brother looked as happy as a loon. Probably because he didn't have a care in the world. Or maybe because things had gone better for Riley with women last night than they had for Finn. "Sorry. Maybe another time. I have a ton of work to do."

"Yeah, yeah." Riley waved that off. "And last I checked you were human…"

Finn dropped his gaze to his hands, his feet, then back up to Riley. "It appears so."

"And that means you need to eat on a regular basis. So come on." Riley waved at him. "Hey, I'll even treat."

Finn chuckled. "Considering that's almost a miracle in the making—"

"Hey." Riley grinned. "I resemble that remark."

"You're the poster child for it." Finn shook his head. Then his stomach rumbled and overruled his work resolve. "All right. You win. But let's make it a quick lunch."

"You know me. I'm always ready to get my nose back to the grindstone. Or rather, ready to get *your* nose back to *your* grindstone, and mine back to lazy living." Riley laughed at his joke, then walked with Finn down the hall to the elevator. "You know it wouldn't hurt you to take a day off once in a while. Maybe even enough time off to have a date or ten."

The doors opened with a soft ding sound and Finn stepped inside, followed by Riley. "We've had this argument before. Last night if I remember right."

"Yep. And we're going to keep having it until you admit I'm right and you're lonely."

"I'm fine." Finn punched the button for the lobby.

"You tell yourself that enough and you might even start to believe it someday, big brother."

Finn ignored the jab. "So how's the waitress?"

"I don't know." Riley shrugged. "I ended up leaving with the brunette."

Finn rolled his eyes.

Riley grinned. "What can I say? The world is filled with beautiful women. Like the one you were supposed to talk to last night. How'd that go?"

"It didn't go quite the way I expected." Had he come on too strong? Too weak? He found himself wondering what she was doing right now. Was Ellie having lunch at her desk? With a friend? Or alone in a restaurant?

She'd been on his mind almost every minute since she'd walked out of the diner. That alone was a clear sign he needed to work more and think less. He wasn't interested in Ellie Winston on a personal basis, even if his hormones were mounting a vocal disagreement.

"What, you struck out? Didn't get her phone number?" Riley asked.

"Her office number is in the yellow pages. I didn't need to ask for that."

Riley shook his head. "And the Hawk strikes again. Always business with you."

The elevator doors shimmied open. Finn and Riley crossed the lobby and exited onto Beacon Street. In the distance, rowers skimmed their sculls down the rippling blue river.

The Hawk strikes again.

Maybe it was the too sunny weather or maybe it was the rejection last night, but Finn found himself bothered by that phrase. He'd never much liked the moniker, but he'd always thought that he, of all people, combined humanity with business. He had never seen himself as quite the cold fish the media depicted.

His brother didn't understand what drove Finn. What kept him at that desk every day. What monumental weights sat on his shoulder, even as he tried to shed them. The one time he'd tried to live a "normal" life, he'd been burned. Badly. More than enough reason not to make that mistake again.

A slight breeze danced across the Charles River, tempering the heat of the day with a touch of cool. They walked for a while, navigating the rush of lunchgoers, heading for the same place they always went, in unspoken agreement. That was one good thing about lunch with Riley—the kind of common mind that came from being siblings. Even though he and Riley were as different as apples and oranges, Finn had always had a closer relationship with him than with Brody. Maybe because Riley was easy to talk to, easy to listen to, and the one who—though he kidded often—understood Finn the best. Even if their minds often moved on opposite tracks.

They reached the shadowed entrance to McGill's.

Finn paused before tugging on the door. "Do you ever wonder…"

Riley glanced at his brother. "Wonder what?"

"Nothing." Finn opened the door and stepped into the air-conditioned interior. The last person he needed to ask for personal—and definitely business—advice was his brother. Riley's standard answer—get a girl, get a room and get busy.

He wanted to ask Riley how his little brother could give his heart so freely. And whether doing so was worth the cost at the end when his heart was broken. He'd seen how much it hurt when the one you were supposed to love no longer felt the same. He had watched that pain erode the happiness in his mother's face day by day. As the youngest, Riley had missed those subtle cues.

Finn shrugged off the thoughts. It had to be the spring weather—and the overabundance of lovey-dovey couples out enjoying the sunshine—that had him feeling so maudlin. He liked his life just the way it was. He didn't need anything more than that.

It took a second for his eyes to adjust to the dim room, and to take in the space. McGill's had a warm interior—dark, rough-hewn plank walls, sturdy, practical tables and chairs and a worn oak floor that had been distressed by thousands of customers' shoes. The food was hearty and good—thick sandwiches, hand-cut fries, stout beer. Finn and Riley came here often, and were waved over to the table area by Steve McGill himself, who was working the bar this afternoon.

Finn waved off the waiter's offer of beer, opting for water instead. "The usual, Marty."

Marty MacDonald had been there for as long as Finn could remember. He had to be nearing seventy, but he moved twice as fast, and had twice the memory of the younger waiters at McGill's. Marty nodded, then turned to Riley. "For you?"

"I'll have my beer, and his. No sense in wasting it." Riley grinned. "And a corned beef sandwich on rye."

Marty chuckled. "In other words, the usual?"

"You know me well, Marty." Riley waited until their server had left, then turned back to Finn. "So what do you think went wrong with the grand plan last night?"

Finn's phone rang. He signaled to Riley to wait a second, then answered the call. "Finn McKenna."

"I wanted to update you on the Langham project," Noel, one of Finn's architects, said. "I heard that Park came in twenty percent lower than us. The client said they're going to go with him instead. Sorry we lost the job, Finn."

Joe Park, a newcomer to Boston's crowded architectural playing field, and someone who often underbid just to get the work. Finn suspected it was the cost savings, and some residual damage to McKenna's reputation that had spurred the client's defection. Finn refused to let another client go.

"No, they won't," he said. "Let me give Langham a call. In five minutes he'll see the wisdom of sticking with us." Finn hung up with Noel, then called the client. In a matter of minutes, he had convinced the penny pinching CEO that working with the established McKenna Designs was a far smarter choice than a rookie newbie. He soothed the worried waters with Langham, and assured him that McKenna Designs would be on top of the project from start to finish. He didn't say anything outright bad about his competitor, but the implication was clear—work with the unproven Park, and the work would be substandard.

After Finn finished the call and put away the phone,

Riley shot him a grin. "I'm glad I'm not one of your competitors."

"It's business, Riley."

"That's not business, that's guerilla warfare." Riley shook his head. "Tell me you didn't treat that gorgeous lady the same way?"

"No, in fact quite the opposite. I think I might have been too nice."

Riley snorted.

"She turned me down. But I'm going to regroup, find another way." Finn reached into the breast pocket of his suit. "I've got a list of pros and cons I'm going to present to her—"

Riley pushed Finn's hand away. "For a smart guy, you can be a complete idiot sometimes."

"This is logical, sound reasoning. Any smart business-person would—"

"I'm sure you're right. And if you have a month or three to go back and forth on pros and cons and hereto-fores and whatevers, I'd agree with you." Riley leaned in closer. "But you don't have that kind of time."

Apparently Riley had been listening to Finn's wor-ries over the past year. Finn was impressed with his lit-tle brother's intuitiveness. Maybe he didn't give Riley enough credit. "True."

"So that means you need to change your tactics."

Finn had an argument ready, but he bit it back. Riley had a point. Negotiations took time, and that was pretty much what his list was. He was an expert when it came to the art of the business deal, but this was different— and he'd struck out with Ellie Winston in a big way. He needed a new idea, and right now, he'd take ideas from about anyone and anywhere. "Okay. How?"

Riley grinned and sat back. "Easy. Do what I do."

"I am not sleeping with her just to get what I want." Finn scowled. "You have a one-track mind."

Riley pressed a hand to his heart. "Finn, you wound me. I would never suggest that. Well, I might, but not in your case." Riley paused. "Especially not in your case."

"Hey."

"You are way too uptight and practical to do such a thing."

"For good reason." Nearly every move in his life was well planned, thought out and executed with precision. Even his relationship with his ex had been like that. He'd chosen a partner who was a peer, someone with common interests, in the right age range and with the kind of quiet understated personality that seemed to best suit his own.

It had seemed to be the wisest choice all around. The kind that wouldn't leave him—or her—unhappy in the end. He'd been stunned when she'd broken up with him and worse, maligned his business and revealed she'd only gone out with him to get information.

But had that been real love? If he could so easily be over the relationship, at least emotionally? Was real love methodical, planned?

Or a wild, heady rush?

The image of Ellie in that figure-hugging maroon dress, her head thrown back in laughter, her eyes dancing with merriment, sent a blast of heat through him. He suspected she was the kind of woman who could get a man to forget a lot more than just his business agenda. For just a second, that empty feeling in his chest lifted. Damn, he really needed to eat more or sleep more or something. He was nearly a blubbering emotional idiot today.

Wild heady rushes didn't mix with business. Wild

heady rushes led to heartache down the road. Wild heady rushes were the exact opposite of Finn McKenna.

"The secret to getting what you want, especially from a woman, is very simple," Riley said.

"Flowers and wine?"

Riley laughed. "That always helps, but no, that's not what I meant."

Marty dropped off their drinks, so quietly they barely noticed his presence. Marty knew them well, and knew when he could interrupt and when to just slip in and out like a cat in the night.

"You find out what the other party wants most in the world," Riley said, "then give it to them."

"That's what my list—"

"Oh, for Pete's sake, Finn. Women aren't into lists and pros and cons. Hell, who is?" Then he paused. "Okay, maybe you. But not the rest of the world. Most people are driven by three needs." He flipped out his fingers and ticked them off as he spoke. "Money, love and sex."

Finn chuckled and shook his head. Riley's advice made sense, in a twisted way. Hadn't Finn done the same thing in business a hundred times? Find out what the other party wants and offer it, albeit with conditions that benefited both sides. "Let me guess. You're driven by number three."

"Maybe." Riley grinned. "One of the three is what drives that pretty little blonde you met with last night. Figure out what it is she wants and give it to her."

"Simple as that?"

Riley sat back and took a sip from his beer. "Simple as that."

The room closed in on her, suddenly too hot, too close. Ellie stared at the woman across from her, letting the words echo in her mind. For a long time, they didn't make sense. It was all a muddled hum of sounds, rattling around in her brain. Then the sounds coalesced one syllable at a time, into a painful reality.

"Are you sure?" Ellie asked. She had walked into this office on a bright Monday morning and now it seemed in the space of seconds, the day had gone dark.

Linda Simpson nodded. "I'm so sorry, Ellie."

She'd know Linda for months, and in that time, Linda had become Ellie's biggest supporter as well as a friend. All these weeks, the news had been positive.

Operative words—*had been.*

Ellie pressed a hand to her belly, and thought of all she had given up to be a woman in a male-dominated field. Relationships…children. Children that now she knew would never happen naturally. Adoption, the obstetrical specialist had told her, was the only option.

Maybe it was her father's illness, or the approach of her thirtieth birthday, but lately, she'd been thinking more and more about the…quiet of her life. For years, she'd been happy living alone, making her own hours, traveling where she wanted. But in the last year or two, there'd been no louder, sadder sound than the echo of her footsteps on tile. She had no one but her father, and if the doctors were right, soon she wouldn't even have him.

And what would she have to show for it? A few dozen houses she'd designed? Houses where other people lived and laughed and raised children and shooed dogs out of the kitchen. Houses containing the very dreams Ellie had pushed to the side.

But no more. Jiao was waiting for her, now stuck in a limbo of red tape at an orphanage in China. Jiao, an energetic two-year-old little girl with wide eyes and dark hair, and a toothy smile. Everything Ellie had dreamed of was right there, within her grasp.

Or had been, until now.

Had Ellie heard wrong? But one look at Linda Simpson's face, lined with sympathy and regret, told Ellie this was no joke. The adoption coordinator sat behind her desk, her dark brown hair piled into a messy bun, her eyes brimming with sorrow.

"I need…" Ellie swallowed, tried again. "A husband?"

"That's what they told me this morning. Countries all over the world are tightening their adoption policies. The orphanage is sticking to the government's bottom line. I'm sorry."

A spouse.

Ellie bit back a sigh. Maybe it was time to pursue another adoption, in a more lenient country. But then she thought of Jiao's round, cherubic face, the laughter that had seemed to fill the room whenever Ellie had played with her, and knew there was nothing she wanted more than to bring that little girl home. She had promised Sun, and Jiao.

But how was she going to do that *and* run her father's company? And who on earth could she possibly marry on such short notice? There had to be a way out of this. A workaround of some sort.

"But they told me, *you* told me, I was fine. That because Jiao's mother asked me specifically to raise her daughter and endorsed the adoption before she died, that I wouldn't have to worry about the other requirements."

"The government is the ultimate authority." Linda spread her hands in a helpless gesture. "And they just feel better about a child being placed in a home with two parents."

Ellie tamped down her frustration. Being mad at

Linda didn't help. The coordinator had worked tirelessly to facilitate this adoption, working with both the U.S. and Chinese governments, as well as the orphanage where Jiao was currently living. Ellie had contacted the agency where Linda worked shortly after returning from that fateful China trip. She'd explained the situation to the woman, who had immediately helped set everything up for a later adoption, easing Sun's worries during the last days of her life.

Ellie had expected some delays, particularly dealing with a foreign government, but already three months had passed since Sun had died and Jiao was still in China.

A husband. Where was she going to get one of those? It wasn't like she could just buy one on the drugstore shelf. Getting married took time, forethought. A relationship with someone.

"What happens now?" Ellie asked. "What happens to Jiao?"

"Well, it would be handy if you had a boyfriend who was looking to commit in the very near future. But if not..." Linda put out her hands again. "I'm sorry. Maybe this one isn't meant to be." Linda didn't have to say anything more. Ellie knew, without hearing the words, that her child would go back into the orphanage system and maybe languish there for years.

Ellie couldn't believe that this wasn't meant to be. Not for a second. The entire serendipitous way she had met Sun, the way the two of them had become instant friends, despite the cultural and language barriers.

And Jiao...

She already loved the little girl. Ellie had held Jiao. Laughed with her. Bonded. During her trips to China, Ellie had become a part of Jiao's little family. A second mother, in a way, to Jiao, who had curled into Ellie and clung to her when they had buried Sun. It had broken Ellie's heart to have to go back to the United States without the little girl. She'd only done it because she'd been assured the next few steps of the adoption were merely a formality.

And now Jiao was all alone in the world, living in a crowded, understaffed orphanage, probably scared and lonely and wondering why she had no family anymore. Ellie thought of Jiao's pixie face, her inquisitive eyes and her contagious smile. Desperation clawed at Ellie. *Oh, God, Jiao. What am I going to do?*

Ellie took a deep breath. Another. She needed to be calm. To think.

Damn it. Ellie had made a promise. Jiao deserved to be raised with security and love, and Ellie would find some way to make that happen. "Let me think about this," she said. "Can I call you later?"

Linda nodded, her warm brown eyes pooling with sympathy. "Sure. I have a day or two to get back to the orphanage."

The unspoken message, though, was that after that, Jiao would slip out of Ellie's grasp like wind through the trees. Off to another family or worse, stuck in the system. Ellie needed a miracle.

And she needed it now.

CHAPTER FOUR

FINN MCKENNA was not a man easily surprised. He'd heard and seen a great deal in the past ten years of running his own company. But this…offer, if that was what he could call it, from Ellie Winston was a total shock.

"Marriage? As in a church and a minister?" he said. The words choked past his throat.

"Well, I was thinking more like city hall and a judge, but if you insist…" She grinned.

"But…w-we don't even know each other." The words sputtered out of him. He, a man who never sputtered.

Ever since she'd walked into his office five minutes ago and announced she had a counteroffer to his, that was what he had done—sputtered. And stammered. And parroted her words back at her. He couldn't believe what he was hearing. *Shocked* wasn't an adequate adjective.

Marriage?

He had expected her to ask for more autonomy with the project or a larger cut of the fee. Something…practical.

Instead she'd said she would allow him to be an equal partner in the Piedmont hospital project, if he married her.

Marriage.

"I think I need a little more time to…think about this."

Or find a counteroffer that could possibly overrule her insane request. "Perhaps we could table this—"

"I'd rather not." She was perched on the edge of one of the visitor's chairs in his office. The late morning sun danced gold in her hair. She had on another dress, this one in a pale yellow that made him think of daffodils.

For Pete's sake. Every time he got close to Ellie Winston he turned into a damned greeting card.

"If you're free for a little while," she added, "how about we go someplace and talk?"

He considered saying no, but then realized this was his best opportunity to get what he needed from Ellie Winston. In the long run, that would serve him better than staying at his desk. It wasn't the fact that he wanted to see more of her. Not at all. He glanced out his window. "We could do lunch, and be stuck in some restaurant or…the weather is gorgeous. How about a stroll on the Esplanade?"

"Sure. I can't remember the last time I walked along the river." She reached into her purse and pulled out a small bag. "I even have flats with me."

"Practical woman."

She laughed. "Sometimes, not so much, but today, yes." She slipped off her heels, tucked them in her bag, then slid on the other shoes.

Finn told Miss Marstein that he was leaving, then shut down his computer and grabbed his phone. A few minutes later, they were out the door and heading down a side street toward the Esplanade. Finn drew in a deep breath of sweet salty air. "I definitely don't get outside enough."

Ellie sighed. "Me, either. When I was younger, I used to be a real outdoorsy girl. Hiking, canoeing, bike riding. I tried to keep up with that after college, but the job takes up way too much time."

He arched a brow at her dress and the spiky heels poking out of her purse. "You hiked?"

Ellie put a fist on her hip. "Do I look too girly for that?"

His gaze raked over her curves, and his thoughts strayed from business to something far more personal. Damn. "Uh, no. Not at all."

"What about you?" she asked. "Do you hike or bike or anything like that?"

"I used to. I ran track in high school, was on the swim team, you name it. And during college, I biked everywhere. Now I think my bike's tires are flat and there are spiders making webs in the frame."

She laughed. "All the more reason to get it out of storage."

They crossed to the Esplanade, joining the hundreds of other people outside. A few on bikes whizzed past them, as if adding an exclamation point to the conversation. "Maybe someday I will," Finn said, watching a man on a carbon fiber racing bike zip past him. "I do miss it."

"Someday might never come," Ellie said quietly. "It's too easy to let the To Do list get in the way. And then before you know it, another year has passed, and another, and you're still sitting behind the desk instead of doing what you love."

He heard something more in her voice. Some kind of longing. Just for more outdoor time? Or to fill another hole in her life? He wanted to ask, wanted to tell her he knew all about using work to plug those empty spots.

But he didn't.

The bike rider disappeared among a sea of power walkers. Finn returned his attention to Ellie. She looked radiant in the sunshine. Tempting. *Too* tempting. He cleared his throat. "It's hard to keep up with the personal To Do list when the business one is so much longer."

"Isn't part of your business taking care of you? After all, if the CEO ain't happy…" She let the words trail off and shot him a grin.

For a second, Finn wanted to fall into that engaging smile of Ellie Winston's. Every one of her smiles seemed to hit him deep in the gut. They were the kind of smiles that Finn suspected—no, knew—would linger in his mind long after they were done. And her voice… her years of living in the South gave her just enough of a Southern tinge to coat her words with a sweet but sassy spin. It was…intoxicating.

Hell, everything about her was intoxicating. It wasn't just the dress or the smile or the curves. It was everything put together, in one unique, intriguing package.

She had him thinking about what it would be like to take a hike through Blue Hills with her, to crest the mountain and watch the busy world go by far beneath them. He imagined them picnicking on a rock outcropping, while the sun warmed their backs and the breeze danced along their skin.

Damn. What was it about her that kept getting him distracted? He needed to focus on business, and more importantly, on why she had proposed marriage a few minutes ago. No wild, heady anything with her.

Finn cleared his throat. "About your…proposal earlier. No pun intended. Were you serious?"

Her features went from teasing to flat, and he almost regretted steering the conversation back. "Yes. Very." She let out a long breath, and for a while, watched the people sitting on the grass across from them. It was a family of four, with a small dog nipping at the heels of the children as they ran a circle around their parents. "I need something from you and you need something from me. Marriage is the best solution all around."

"We could always do a legal agreement for the businesses. This is just one project, you know."

"For me, it's much more." Her gaze returned to his. "I have to have a husband. Now."

"Why?"

"First, let me lay out the advantages to you." She slowed her pace. "For one, our lack of familiarity with each other is what makes it a perfect idea and a perfect partnership, if you will."

"Partnership, perhaps. Not a marriage."

"I may not know you very well, Mr. McKenna," she went on, "but I know your life. You work sunup to sundown, travel half the year and have all the social life of a barnacle."

She could have opened up his skull and peeked inside his brain. Damn. Was he that transparent? And put that way, well, hell, his life sounded downright pitiful. Riley would have put up two enthusiastic thumbs in agreement.

Perhaps she was joking. He glanced at her face. Saw only serious intent in her features.

"But don't you think it's wiser to work out a business arrangement instead? More money, more prestige, a reciprocal arrangement with my next project?" Something he could quantify, put into those neat little debits and credits columns. Not something like *marriage*, for Pete's sake.

"Perhaps to you it would be. But a business arrangement isn't the number one thing I need right now." She gestured toward a small grassy hill that led to the river, away from the crowds out walking, and the energetic inline skaters rushing past them. He followed her down to the water's edge. In the distance, a rowing team called out a cadence as they skimmed across the glassy blue surface.

Her green eyes met his, and a thrill ran through him. Damn, she had beautiful eyes.

"Not to mention, you're probably as tired of the dating game as am I," she said. "And maybe you've looked ahead to the future, and wondered how on earth you're going to fit the American Dream into your schedule."

He gave her a droll smile. "Actually I had that down for next year, on Tuesday, March 30, at two in the afternoon."

She burst out laughing, which also surprised him and stirred that warmth again in his gut. Those who knew Finn would never have described him as a man with a sense of humor. But apparently Ellie Winston found him funny. That pleased him, and had him wondering what else Ellie thought of him.

Damn. He kept getting off track. It had to be her proposal which had knocked the normally unflappable Finn off balance.

"I was hoping to fit it into my planner a little sooner than that," she said. "Actually a lot sooner."

"Why? Why now? And…why me? I mean, you are a beautiful woman. Smart, charming, sexy. You could have your pick of any man on the planet."

"I…well, thank you." Now it was her turn to sputter. A soft pink blush spread over her cheeks. Then she paused, seeming to weigh her answer for several moments before responding. He got the distinct impression she was holding something back, but what, he didn't know. He thought again about what he knew about her. Nothing pointed to "desperate to get married," no matter how he looked at the details he knew about her. Yet, there was an ulterior motive to her proposal—he'd bet a year's salary on it.

"There's a child in China who needs a mother. I promised her that I would adopt her, and everything was in place for me to do so. Until this morning." She bit her lip and turned to him. "The agency told me I need a husband to complete the adoption."

"Whoa, whoa." He put up his hands. "I'm not interested in becoming an instant father."

"I'm not asking that of you. At all."

"Then what *are* you asking?"

"A marriage based on commonality, not passion or lust or infatuation. We'll stay married for a short time, long enough for me to get the adoption finalized, then get a quiet divorce. Painless and fast."

In other words, no real strings attached and he'd be out of this nearly as fast as he was in it. He should be glad. For some reason, he wasn't. "Sounds so…clinical."

"Mr. McKenna…Finn. We're both detail oriented—clinical in a way—people. I'm not interested in losing my head in a relationship, or wasting a lot of time dating Mr. Wrong, not when I'm concentrating on running my father's company. I need a spouse, in name only, and you need a business partner."

He looked in Ellie Winston's eyes, and saw only sincerity, and a quiet desperation to help a child halfway around the world. He knew she wouldn't have come to him, with this insane offer, if she didn't have to.

Find out what she wants most in the world, Riley had said, and give it to her.

But this?

"I don't know if I agree with this," Finn said. "The child will undoubtedly be hurt when her father disappears after a few weeks."

"You don't have to be a part of Jiao's life at all. Just be there for the home visit and the adoption proceedings. And in return, we can work together on the Piedmont project. That will keep my father's business growing and help yours. It's a win all around."

Pigeons picked at the grass before them, looking for leftover crumbs. In the distance, there was the sound of children's laughter. The swish-swish of rolling cycle tires on the paved walkway. The continual hum of traffic, punctuated by the occasional horn. The world went on as it always did, swimming along beneath a sunny sky.

"It would be a platonic marriage," she said. "Nothing more."

"A purely impersonal alliance?" he asked, still not believing she had suggested this. When he'd made his list of possible ways to convince Ellie a strategic partnership was a good idea, marriage hadn't even come close to being in the mix. "A marriage based solely on like minds and like goals?"

Though when he put the marriage idea like that, it sounded cold. Almost…sad.

He shook off the thoughts. He was a practical man. One whose focus was solely on building his business back to where it had been. He wasn't going to get wrapped up in the foolishness of some romantic ideal— and that wasn't what Ellie was asking for. It was, in fact, the exact kind of relationship he had vowed to pursue. Then why did he feel as empty as a deflated balloon?

She nodded. "Yes."

"And in exchange, our companies partner as well?"

"Yes." She put up a finger. "However, we each retain ownership and leadership of our respective companies, in case…things don't work out." She dug in her purse and pulled out a piece of paper. "I took the liberty of having my attorney draw up a contract."

A contract. For marriage.

Finn skimmed the document and saw that it indeed promised everything she had talked about. The business arrangement, the annulment agreement. All he had to do was sign on the dotted line and he'd be a temporary husband, father in name only.

The businessman in him said it was an opportunity not to be missed. The partnership his business needed, and at the same time, the bonus of companionship. Not sex, clearly, but someone to talk to at the end of the day.

He thought of the nights he'd spent on the rooftop deck of his townhouse. Watching the city lights twinkle in the distance, while he drank a beer, and gathered his thoughts, wondered if he'd made the right choices. Lately those nights hadn't brought the peace they used to. More, a restlessness, a question of "is this all there is?" Except for the times he was with his brothers, his life was staid. Almost dull.

Riley was right. He was lonely, and tired as hell of feeling that way.

At the same time, he didn't want to pursue the empty one-night stands his brother did. He wanted more, something with meaning and depth. Something that was... sensible. Reliable. Practical. Something that wasn't foolish or wild or crazy—not the kind of whirlwind romance his parents had had, that had gone so horribly wrong after the children started coming and they realized that a quick courtship couldn't build a lifetime, not between such badly mismatched people.

Love—or any approximation of it—was a dangerous thing that left a man vulnerable. Not a position Finn

McKenna relished or welcomed. A marriage of convenience would be void of all those things.

Still, the cynic in him wondered if Ellie was proposing this as a way to knock him off guard, or maybe even an alliance that would allow her to gather facts about him and his business, facts she could use to take over his company later or eliminate him as a competitor. Hadn't Lucy done exactly the same thing?

But the man in him, the one standing beside a very beautiful, very intriguing woman with a smile that stayed with him, hoped like hell it was something more than that.

Was he truly considering this…this marriage of convenience? What choice did he have? He needed to be a part of that hospital project. Making it a joint venture with a company like WW would reestablish his company's reputation, and distract attention from that fiasco last year. And, as calculated as it sounded, a marriage to a charming woman like Ellie would also distract attention from the mess his company had been in lately, give the gossips something else to talk about. He'd be back on top before he knew it, and then he and Eleanor Winston could quietly dissolve the union, as she'd said. She'd have the child, and he'd have his business back. He could feel the old familiar surge of adrenaline that always hit him when he landed a big job, one that he knew could change the future of McKenna Designs.

"This contract looks pretty good," he said.

"I wanted to make it clear this was business only." Her gaze flicked to the water, and she let out a small sigh. Almost like she was disappointed. Which was crazy, because she was the one floating the idea in the first place. "But we don't have a lot of time to waste. Jiao is stuck in that orphanage, farther away from me with every pass-

ing day. And you, I suspect, would like to be on board
from day one with the hospital project. The initial drawings are due the fifteenth so we have very little time to
get everyone up to speed."

"The fifteenth? That does put a crunch on our time.
By all rights, we should start right away."

"I agree. In the end, Finn, we're both decisive people, aren't we?" She smiled at him. "I'm not looking for
a courtship with flowers and dancing and dinners out.
What we are doing is more of a…"

"Partnership. Two like minds coming together."

"Exactly."

A part of him felt a whisper of…loss? Finn wasn't
sure that was the right word to describe the yawning
emptiness in his gut. Surely a deal like this—one that
would benefit his company and at the same time, fill
those quiet, lonely nights with good conversation, was
a win-win all around.

Except…

No, he didn't need any more than that. As Ellie had
said, a romantic relationship came with complications,
emotional drama—all things he didn't have time for,
nor wanted in his life. And clearly, not something she
wanted, either. She saw him as a means to an end, and
he saw her the same way.

Hadn't he learned his lesson with Lucy? A heady relationship would do nothing but draw his attention away
from the business. In the coming months, the company
would need more of his attention than ever, so the kind
of relationship Ellie was proposing was perfect. With
the addition of the legal contract, the risk to McKenna
Designs would be minimal. He saw no downside to this.

Except the fact that it wouldn't be a real marriage.
That it would be as faux as the wood paneling that still

flanked his grandmother's fireplace, forty years after the house had been built, the same house she lived in because it was the one she'd bought with her late husband, even though she could now afford ten times the house.

A hummingbird flitted by, heading for a bright swath of flowers. Finn watched it for a while, as the world hustled by behind him.

"There's this bird in Africa," Finn said, watching the tiny hummingbird dart from bloom to bloom, "called a honey guide. Its whole job is to find beehives and lead the honey badger to them. When he does, the badger gets in there and gets the honey, clearing the way for the honey guide to eat the bee larvae." He turned to Ellie. "I guess that's sort of what this will be. Us working together to serve a mutually beneficial purpose."

"Not exactly the same as swans mating for life, but yes."

"Definitely not a partnership for life," Finn said. But even as he clarified, he felt a twinge of something like regret. He shrugged it off. Be smart, he reminded himself, like the badger and the bird. In the end, everyone wins.

"I don't want to rush you," she said. "But we need to make a decision. If you don't want to do this…I need to think of something else."

"Fine," he said, turning to her. "Let's go."

She blinked. "What…now?"

"Why wait?" he said, parroting her words back. "I have a friend at the courthouse. He'll take care of it. You can be my wife by the end of the day, Miss Winston."

"Today? Right now?"

"Yes, of course." He watched her closely, and wondered if, despite the contract she'd given him, she was as committed to this partnership as she had sounded. Only one way to find out, he decided. "You weren't expecting me to get down on one knee with some flowers or a ring, were you?"

"No, no, of course not." She swallowed. "Business only."

"My favorite kind of relationship." He gave her a smile, then turned to go back across the grass. He paused, turned back, waiting for her to join him. He had called Ellie Winston's bluff. The only problem...

He wasn't so sure she'd been bluffing.

"Are you ready?"

Was she ready? Ellie had no idea if she was or wasn't. The events of the last hours seemed surreal, as if it was some other Ellie Winston who had proposed to Finn McKenna, then hopped in his Town Car and headed to Rhode Island in the middle of the day.

Had she really just proposed to him? And had he really accepted?

She'd gone to his office right after leaving the adoption agency and then her lawyer's office, her mind filled with only one thing. She needed a husband and she needed one now. She'd do whatever it took to get that. She'd seen Jiao's trusting, hopeful face in her mind and thought of nothing else. Jiao needed a mother. Needed Ellie.

Linda had made it clear—marriage was the only sure route to bringing Jiao home. There was no one else that Ellie knew—not well enough in her short time living here in Boston—who would marry her on such short notice. No one who would go along with such a crazy plan, and not expect a real marriage out of the deal. So she'd gone to Finn, the only man she knew who needed her as much as she needed him.

A part of her had never expected him to say yes. But

say yes, he had, and now they were on their way to get married.

Married.

To Finn McKenna.

A man she knew about as well as she knew her dry cleaner.

This was insane. Think of Jiao, she told herself. Just think of Jiao. And as the miles ticked by, that became her mantra.

Massachusetts had a three-day waiting period for a marriage license, Finn had told her, as he got on I-95S and made the hour-long journey to Providence, Rhode Island, where there was no waiting period. The car's smooth, nearly silent ride and comfortable interior made the whole drive seem almost…romantic, even though it was broad daylight and the highway was filled with other cars. It was something about the cozy, dark leather of the car that wrapped around her, insulated them, drew them into a world of just the two of them, like lovers making an afternoon getaway. Which was crazy, because what they were doing was far from romantic. And they were definitely not lovers.

"How did you know there was a three-day waiting period in Massachusetts?" she asked.

"My brother." A grin slid across Finn's face. "Riley is a little…impetuous. We've had to talk him out of more than one crazy decision."

"We?"

"My younger brother Brody and me. We're the ones who received all the common-sense genes."

"Inherited from generations of common-sense McKenna men?"

He chuckled. "Exactly. Though my grandmother might quibble with how much common sense is in our DNA."

"So there are three of you altogether?" Ellie asked.

"Yep. All boys. Made for a busy life. Hell, it still does."

She tried to picture that environment, with three rambunctious, noisy siblings, and couldn't. The camaraderie. The joking. The warmth. "I'm an only child. I can't even imagine what it would be like to grow up with two sisters, or a bunch of brothers."

"It's loud. And sometimes things get broken." Finn put up a hand and pressed three fingers together. "Scouts' Honor, I had nothing to do with that antique vase or the missing coffee table."

Ellie heard the laughter buried in Finn's voice and craved those same kinds of memories for Jiao. She bit back a sigh. Adopting just one child as a single mother was proving to be difficult enough. Adopting multiple children seemed impossible. But maybe someday—

She'd have the warm, crazy, boisterous family Finn was describing.

Except that would mean taking a risk and falling in love. Ellie didn't need to complicate her life with a relationship that could end up hurting her—and in the process her daughter—down the road. This marriage, based on a legal contract and nothing else, was the best choice.

"Remind me to tell you the tree story sometime," Finn said. "And every year at Thanksgiving, we revisit the Ferris wheel one. That one was all Riley's fault. There's always an interesting story where Riley is concerned, and Brody and I try to exploit that at every opportunity."

Her gaze went to the city passing by outside the window, streaks of color in the bright sunshine. Thanksgivings and Christmases with a whole brood of McKenna men sounded like heaven, Ellie thought. Her childhood had been so quiet, so empty, with her mother gone all the time and her father working sunup to sundown. She envied Finn and for a moment, wondered if they would be married long enough for her to sit around the Thanksgiving dinner table with a trio of McKennas, sharing raucous stories and building memories over the turkey.

She pictured that very thing for a moment, then pulled away from the images. They were a bird and a badger, as he'd pointed out, not two swans in love. Besides, she knew better than to pin her hopes on some romantic notion of love. That happened for other people, not her.

"My parents weren't around much when I was a kid. Now my mother lives in California, so it's really just my dad and me." She shifted in her seat to look at him. "I guess you could say my life has always been pretty… quiet and predictable." Now that she said it, she wondered if that was such a good thing. For one, she wanted to add the chaos of a child. Would she be ready for it? She, who had never so much as babysat a neighbor's kid? Save for a few vacations spent in China with Jiao and Sun, she had no experience with children…what made her think she could do this? Heck, Finn, with all those younger brothers, was probably better suited to parenting than she was.

All Ellie had was a deep rooted conviction that she would love her child and be there for her. She wouldn't leave Jiao with an endless stream of babysitters or miss her third-grade recital or pay a tutor to help her with her homework so Ellie could work a few more hours. She would be there.

Somehow, she'd find a way to run WW Designs and be the mother that Jiao needed, the kind of parent Ellie had never had. Even though she knew it would be easier to do that if she had a real husband, one who was a plugged-in father, she vowed to make this work on her own. One attentive, loving parent was better than two inattentive, unavailable parents. And she had no intentions of forcing this marriage to limp along after the adoption was final. The worst thing for Jiao would be to have a distant parent, one who left her wondering if she was truly loved.

Finn turned on his blinker, then exited the highway. "Your life might have been quiet and predictable up until now, but I'd say getting married on the spur of the moment is pretty far from either of those adjectives."

She laughed. "You're right. No one would ever think I'd elope."

"That goes double for me." Finn paused at the end of the off-ramp. He turned to face her, his blue eyes hidden by dark sunglasses. "Still sure you want to do this?"

She thought of what he had just told her. About his brothers and his noisy childhood. Then thought of the quiet, empty life she led. She had her father, yes, but other than that, all she had was work.

"Yes, I'm sure," she said.

"Okay." Then he made the turn, following the signs that led to the downtown area. "Me, too."

He said it so softly, she wondered if there was more behind the words than a simple agreement. Was he missing something in his life, too? Was he looking to fill the empty spaces, add life to those quiet rooms? Or was this solely a business merger for him?

He said nothing more, just drove, and she let the silence fill the space between them in the cavernous Town Car. A little while later, they pulled in front of the courthouse, a massive brick building with dozens of tall windows and a spire reaching toward the clouds. The stately building resembled a church as much as it did a place for justice.

They parked in one of the many parking garages nearby, then walked the short distance to the court. Ellie noticed that Finn opened her car door, opened the garage's door, lightly took her elbow when they crossed a street. Such small gestures, but ones that Ellie appreciated. After all, this was a business deal. He didn't have to play the chivalrous man.

They went up the few stone steps to the entrance, with Finn stepping in front of her to open and hold the heavy courthouse door for her, too. "Thank you."

"It's the least I can do for my future wife."

She faltered at the word. She'd heard it twice already today, and still couldn't believe it was happening. "Are you planning on carrying me over the threshold, too?"

He paused. "We hadn't talked about that detail."

"Which one?"

"Where we're going to live after this."

The mirth left her. Oh, yeah.

She hadn't thought that far ahead. In fact, she'd just gone with this insane plan, clearly not thinking it through. The adoption agency would undoubtedly do its due diligence before signing off on Ellie's adoption. At the very least, they'd want a report from Linda on the living conditions.

It wouldn't take a genius to realize her marriage was a sham if she and new "husband" were living in separate homes. Ellie had never been much of an impetuous woman. Until today and now, she could lose it all by not thinking this through.

"We should live together," she said, all the while watching for his reaction, "or no one will believe it's real. We'll need people to believe we're together for more than just a business deal."

"We'll have to make it seem…real," he said.

"Yeah. We will."

Finn turned to her in the bright, expansive lobby. People rushed around them, hurrying to courtrooms and offices, their shoes echoing on the marble floors, their voices carrying in the vast space.

But Ellie barely noticed. She stood in a world of only two, herself and the man who had agreed to marry her and in the process, change her life. And Jiao's, too.

"Maybe if people find out I eloped, it'll change their image of me as the Hawk."

She laughed. "And what, turn you into the Dove?"

"I don't think so." He chuckled. "I could get married at a drive-thru chapel in Vegas with Elvis as my best man and that still wouldn't be enough to do that."

"You never know. Marriage changes people. Relationships change them." Her voice was soft, her mind on one person a world away.

"Yes, I think it does. And not always for the better."

She wanted to ask him what he meant by that. Did he mean the ex-fiancée who had ruined his reputation? Or was he talking about something, someone else?

He cleared his throat. "You're right. Our marriage is going to need a measure of verisimilitude, and being in the same residence will do that. In addition, we can work on the hospital project after hours."

Even though Finn's voice was detached, almost clinical, the words *after hours* conjured up thoughts of very different nocturnal activities. Since the first time she'd spotted Finn in the ballroom of the Park Plaza, she'd been intrigued. She'd liked how he bucked convention by having a beer instead of wine, how he'd been so intent yet also charming. From a distance, she'd thought he was handsome. Up close, he was devastating. Her heart skipped a beat every time he smiled. Her traitorous mind flashed to images of Finn touching her, kissing her, making love to her—

Whoa. That was not part of the deal. At all. Keeping this platonic was the only—and best—way to ensure that she could walk away at the end. She didn't want to chance her heart on love, or risk her future with a relationship that could dissolve as easily as sugar in hot tea. Falling for him would only complicate everything.

And marrying him on the spur of the moment wasn't complicated? All of a sudden, a flutter of nerves threatened to choke her. Ellie opened her mouth to tell Finn this was crazy, she couldn't do this, when the door to the courthouse opened behind them and a slim, tall man hurried inside.

"Sorry I'm late. My day has been crazy." He chuckled. "As usual. Story of my life. And yours, too, huh, Finn?"

Finn patted the other man on the back and gave him a grin. "Charlie, how are you?"

"Just fine. Not as good as you, though. Running off to get married. You surprise me, old friend." He grinned, then put out a hand toward Ellie. "Judge Charlie Robinson, at your service."

Ellie gaped. "You said you had a friend in the courthouse. Not a judge."

"Charlie and I have been friends since we were kids. We roomed together at Harvard," Finn said, then shot Charlie a smirk. "To me, he's not a judge. He's the guy who sprayed whipped cream all over my room."

"Hey, I'm still pleading innocent to that one." Charlie raised his hands in a who-me gesture, but there was a twinkle in his eye.

Again, Ellie saw another side of Finn. A side that intrigued her, even as she pushed those thoughts away. She refused to fall for Finn. Now or later. She was here for a practical reason and no other.

Finn chuckled. "Well, we should get to it. I know you have a hectic day."

"No problem. I can always make time for a good friend, especially one who's getting married. So…" Charlie clapped his hands together. "You two kids ready to make this all legal and binding?"

Legal. Binding.

Now.

Ellie glanced at Finn. She could do this. She *had* to. There was no other way. Besides, it was a temporary marriage, nothing more than a piece of paper. But a union that would bring Jiao home and give Ellie the family she had always craved. She could do that, without getting her heart tangled in the process. "Yes," she said.

"Great." Charlie grinned again. "Okay, lovebirds, let's head up to my office and get you two hitched."

Finn turned to Ellie and put out his arm. "Are you ready to become Mrs. McKenna?"

Was she?

She lifted her gaze to Finn's blue eyes. She barely knew this man, but what she knew she liked. Respected. Trusted. Would that be enough?

She thought of Jiao again, and realized it would have to be. In the end, running WW would be fulfilling, but not nearly as fulfilling as coming home to Jiao's contagious smile and wide dark eyes.

"Why, Mr. McKenna, I can't think of another thing I'd rather do in the middle of the day." Then she linked her arm in Finn's and headed toward the judge's chambers.

CHAPTER FIVE

THE whole thing took only a few minutes—including Charlie's beginning jokes and closing quips. They called in his assistant and a court clerk to serve as witnesses, the two of them looking like they'd seen more than one impromptu wedding. Charlie thought they were getting married out of love, and in typical Charlie fashion, strove to make the event fun and memorable. Finn stumbled when Charlie asked him about rings, which Charlie racked up as bridegroom nerves. "I can't believe you, of all people, forgot a major detail like the rings," Charlie said. "No worries, but be sure you make it up to her later with a *lot* of diamonds," he said with a wink, then in the next breath pronounced them man and wife.

Man and wife. The words echoed in Finn's mind, bouncing around like a rubber ball. He'd done it. And no one was more surprised than Finn himself. He, the man who hadn't operated without a plan since he was writing his first research paper in fourth grade, had run off in the middle of the day and—

Eloped.

Holy cow. He'd really done it.

"And now for the best part," Charlie said, closing the book in his hands and laying it on his desk. "You may kiss your bride."

Finn stared at Charlie for a long second. Kiss the bride? He'd forgotten all about that part. He'd simply assumed a quick civil union in a courthouse would be devoid of all the flowers and romance part of a church wedding. "Uh, I don't know if we have to—"

Charlie laughed. "What, are you shy now? Go on, kiss her."

Finn considered refusing, but then thought better of it. Charlie would undoubtedly question a marriage where the groom didn't want to get close with his bride. And if they were going to pull off this fiction in front of their friends and colleagues, they needed to at least look the part. Finn turned to Ellie. Her green eyes were wide, her lips parted slightly. In shock? Anticipation?

She looked beautiful and delicious all at the same time in that simple daffodil-colored dress. In that instant, his reservations disappeared, replaced by a fast, hot surge of want. No, it was more than desire, it was a…craving for whatever inner happiness was lighting Ellie's features.

She stood there, looking as hesitant as he felt. A faint blush colored her cheeks, disappeared beneath her long blond hair. She looked like a bride—pretty, breathless, yet at the same time she possessed a simmering sensuality. He wanted her, even as he reminded himself this was a purely platonic union.

There would be no kisses. No lovemaking. Nothing but this moment. And right now, Finn didn't want to let this moment pass.

Her gaze met his and a curious tease filled the emerald depths. "Well, Mr. McKenna, are you going to do as the nice judge says?"

"I would never disobey a judge," Finn said, his voice low, hoarse. Just between them. Charlie, the witnesses, hell, the entire world ceased to exist.

He closed the gap between them, reached a hand to cup her jaw. Electricity crackled in the air, in the touch. A breath extended between them, another. Ellie's chest rose, fell. Her dark pink lips parted, her deep green eyes widened, and her light floral perfume teased at his senses, luring him closer, closer.

Damn, he wanted her. He'd wanted her from the minute he'd met her.

With one kiss he'd seal this marriage. But was that all this kiss was about? This moment?

No. He knew, deep in his gut, that there was something else happening here, something he wasn't sure he wanted or needed in his life. He could have been standing at the edge of a cliff, ready to plunge—

Into the cushion of water, or the danger of rocks? He didn't know.

All he could feel was this insistent *want*. For her. For just one taste. He lowered his mouth to hers, and at the instant that his lips met hers, he knew.

Knew that kissing Ellie was going to change everything.

Her lips were sweet and soft beneath his, her hair a silky tickle against his fingers. She leaned into him for one long, blissful second, and he inhaled, drawing in the scent of her, memorizing it, capturing the moment in Technicolor in his mind.

Ellie.

Then she drew back and the kiss was over, nearly as quickly as it began. The flush in her cheeks had deepened to a light crimson. Her gaze met his for one hot, electric second, then she looked away, and turned back to Charlie.

Platonic. Business relationship. The heady rush gone.

He told himself he was glad. That it was exactly what he wanted.

"There. It's official now." Charlie grinned, then he reached out and shook hands with both of them. The witnesses murmured their congratulations before slipping out the door. "Congratulations," Charlie said. "May you have an abundance of happiness and children."

Children. Or, rather, a single child. Half the reason they'd embarked on this fake union. Finn glanced over at Ellie, but her gaze was on the window, not on him, hiding whatever she might have thought about Charlie's words.

A few minutes later, they left the courthouse, a newly minted marriage license in hand. The paper weighed nothing, but felt heavier than a concrete block.

Married. To a near stranger.

A stranger whose kiss had awakened a roaring desire inside Finn. He had thought he was doing this just for business reasons, but that kiss was as far from business as the earth was from the moon. And he needed to remember his uppermost goal.

Don't get involved. Don't fall for her. Don't lose track of the priority. Don't get swept up in a tsunami that would leave him worse off in the end.

As they walked down the street toward the parking garage, Finn dug his car keys out of his pocket, then paused. They were married. And that meant the occasion, even if it was merely a professional alliance, deserved some kind of celebration. "How about we get some dinner before we head back to Boston?"

"I should probably get back to work. I left in the middle of my day and have a lot on my To Do list." She stepped to the side to allow a quartet of lunch workers to power past them. "But thanks for the offer."

His To Do list was probably just as long, but for the

first time in a long time, Finn didn't want to go back to his office, didn't feel like sitting behind that mahogany desk, even as the sensible side of him mounted a vigorous objection. "It's not every day you get married, you know. We should at least have a glass of wine to celebrate. Or iced tea for you. I'll have the wine."

"Don't you have work to get to, too?"

"Always. But it's waited this long. It can wait a little longer. Regardless of why we got married, this is a big moment for both of us." He grinned. "Don't you agree?"

It was Finn's smile that swayed Ellie. There was something…disarming about the way Finn McKenna smiled. He had a crooked smile, curving up higher on one side of his face than the other. She liked that. Liked the way nothing about him was exactly what you would expect.

Neither was his kiss. She'd thought that he would just give her a perfunctory peck on the lips, a token gesture to seal the deal. But he'd done so much more. Kissed her in a way she hadn't been kissed in forever.

Their kiss had been short, but tender. When he'd touched her jaw, he'd done it almost reverently, his fingers drifting over her cheek, tangling in her hair. He'd leaned in, captured her gaze and waited long enough for her heart to begin to race with anticipation before he'd kissed her. When had a man ever taken such time for something so simple?

It left her wondering what it would be like to really be Finn's wife. Would he kiss her like that at the end of every day? Before he left for work in the morning? For just a moment, she wanted to hold on to that fantasy, to believe that this was real, and not just a means to an end.

Even if it was.

Finn was right—it wasn't every day that she got married, and she wasn't sure she was quite ready to go back to her ordinary world, and all the questions this was bound to raise. They still had to settle on their story, and deal with other practical issues, like where they were going to live afterward.

Whatever little thrill she might have felt faded in the light of reality. This wasn't a date, it wasn't a celebration. It was business, pure and simple.

And nothing more.

"You did what?" The shock in Riley's voice boomed across the phone connection. *"You got married?"*

"Uh, yeah, but it's not…" Finn was about to tell Riley it wasn't a real marriage, then he glanced across the sidewalk at Ellie, standing in the shadowed circle beneath an oak tree. She was talking into her cell phone with someone at her office, her hand moving to punctuate her words. Little bits of sunshine dappled her blond hair, kissed her delicate features and gave her a slight glow.

He had seen hundreds of beautiful women in his lifetime, but none that had that whole package of incredible looks and incredible personality. The kind of woman any man in his right mind would be proud to call his wife.

Except, this was merely a way to resurrect his business. Besides, he didn't need the complication of a relationship, the heady distraction of a romance. He liked his life as straight as a ruler. And he'd continue to keep it that way.

"It's unexpected, is what it is," Riley finished for him. "What were you thinking?"

"I wasn't." That was true. He'd thought he was challenging her offer, then once they were standing in front of Charlie, he'd stopped thinking about the pros and cons of what he was about to do and just…done it. Eloped. He, of all people. He hadn't thought about the incongruity of that when he was in Charlie's office. All he'd seen was Ellie's smile.

"I thought you were all antimarriage. Especially after the Lucy thing."

"I was. I am. This was…" Finn paused. "Different."

"Well, congratulations, brother," Riley said. "You'll be all the talk at the next family reunion."

Finn chuckled. "I'm sure I will be as soon as you get off the phone and call Brody. You spread gossip faster than a church picnic."

Riley laughed with him. "So, where are you guys going on your honeymoon?"

The word *honeymoon* conjured up images of Ellie's lithe, beautiful body beside his. He glanced at her across the way from him, and didn't see the daffodil-yellow dress, but instead saw her on some beach somewhere. Her skin warmed from the sun, all peaches and cream and pressed against him. Taking things far beyond a simple kiss in the judge's chambers.

Damn. That was not productive. At all. He shook his head, but the images stayed, chased by the memory of kissing her. The scent of her perfume. The feel of her in his arms.

Again, he forced them away and tore his gaze away from Ellie.

He'd come close to that kind of craziness when he'd dated Lucy. Granted, most of their relationship had been practical, staid…predictable. Then he'd had that moment of insanity when he'd rushed out to buy a ring, run over to her office to propose—

And found out she was stealing his clients behind his back.

No more of that. He'd gone off the rails for five minutes, and it nearly destroyed his business and his career.

A smart man approached marriage like any other business deal—with clarity, sense and caution.

"Uh, we don't really have time for that right now," Finn said, reminding himself that there would be no honeymoon. Not now, not later. "Work schedules, meetings, that kind of thing gets in the way of the best laid plans, you know?" He made light of it because for some reason, he couldn't bring himself to tell Riley the whole thing was a temporary state. That most likely by the time their schedules opened up enough that they could plan a joint vacation, they would be filing for divorce.

"You *are* going to celebrate at least a little, aren't you? I mean, if any occasion screams having a party, this is it." Riley paused a second. "Hmm…I wonder if it's too late to throw you a bachelor party?"

"I don't need one of those, and yes, it is too late." Finn shifted the phone in his grasp. "Actually that's why I called you. I was thinking of taking her out for drinks and dinner. But…"

"You realized that idea sounds about as lame as a picnic in the park?"

"Hey!" Then Finn lowered his voice. "What's lame about a picnic?"

Riley laughed. "Don't tell me. That was your second idea."

Finn didn't want to admit that it had actually been his first idea, but then he'd thought about bugs and sunshine, and proposed a restaurant instead. Damn. He was a hell of a lot rustier at this dating game than he'd thought. Not that this was a date—at all—just his effort to make this business alliance a little more palatable. "It's a nice day. We could grab some sandwiches—"

"Last I checked, you don't get married every day. So don't do an everyday thing to celebrate it. Here's what

I would do," Riley said, then detailed a plan for Finn that far surpassed anything Finn had thought of. A few minutes later, Riley said goodbye and Finn ended the call. At the same time, Ellie tucked her phone away and crossed to Finn.

"Sorry about that," she said. "Duty calls."

Finn chuckled. "Believe me, I understand. It calls me all the time, day and night." At the same moment, Finn's phone began to ring. He fished it out of his pocket, about to answer, when Ellie laid a hand on top of his.

"Don't." Her fingers danced lightly across his, an easy, delicate touch, but one that sent a shock wave running down his arm. "Let's put our phones away. I don't want to deal with work for now."

"Me, either." He pressed the power button, turned the phone off, then slipped it into his jacket pocket. "Besides, I have plans for you, Mrs. McKenna."

Her eyes widened at the use of her married name. "Plans? What kind of plans?"

"You'll see," he said, then said a little prayer that he could execute Riley's plans as well as his brother would have. Because just for today, Finn wanted to woo the woman who was now his wife.

Tomorrow was soon enough to get back to business— and stay there. For as long as this practical, contracted arrangement lasted.

How he'd done it, Ellie didn't know. She stared in wonder at the tableau laid out before her. Chubby terra cotta pots held thick, lush flowering shrubs, lit from above by soft torch lights on bronze poles. A pair of squat white wicker chairs with fluffy striped cushions flanked either side of a matching table, already set for dinner with floral plates and crystal wine goblets. Candles flickered in the soft breeze, dropping a blanket of golden light over everything.

The sun had started setting, casting Boston's skyline in a soft purple glow. Lights twinkled in the distance, while the red and green bow lights of passing boats dotted the harbor.

She'd had no idea that Finn had been planning this while they were riding back from Providence. Or how. They had kept their phones off, as agreed, and spent the hour of travel talking about everything and nothing—from growing up in the city to the challenges of architectural design in a world going green.

She'd learned that Finn hated spinach but loved the Red Sox, that he had his one and only B in seventh grade Science and that his first job had been delivering newspapers. She'd told him that her favorite food was cake, and that she'd been the last on her block to learn to ride a bike. She told him about the time she'd gotten lost in the train station and the day she got her braces.

It was the most she'd shared with anyone in a long, long time, and it had felt nice. Then the car pulled up in front of Finn's building and Finn had turned to her and said, "All those details should really help when we meet with the adoption people," and Ellie had been reminded that her marriage was nothing more than a sham.

If that was so, why had Finn gone to all this trouble to set up such a romantic tableau?

"How…when…" She let out a breath. "This is incredible, Finn."

He grinned. "Thank you."

"How did you do it?"

"Remember that rest stop we went to on the way back from Rhode Island?"

She nodded.

"I made a few phone calls while you were…indisposed."

"A few fast phone calls. And clearly productive."

"I'm a man who likes to get things done." He reached for her hand, and she let that happen, wondering when touching Finn had become so easy or if she was just telling herself it was to preserve the mood, and then they walked forward onto the private terrace of his building, temporarily transformed into an outdoor dining room.

Just as Finn pulled out her chair, music began, a soft jazz floating from an unseen sound system. A waiter emerged from a door at the side, bearing a tray with water glasses and a carafe filled with two bottles—one a chilled white wine, the other a sparkling grape juice. He placed the water glasses on the table with merely a nod toward Ellie, then uncorked the wine and juice, pouring Ellie's nonalcoholic version first, then Finn's wine, before disappearing back through the door again. Finn had remembered she didn't drink, and had clearly put a lot of time and thought into the entire evening. Why?

He raised his glass and tilted it toward her. "To… partnership."

"Partnership," she echoed, and ignored the flutter of disappointment in her gut. In the end, they would go their separate ways, and for that, Ellie was glad. She didn't need the complication of dating Finn, of a relationship. Just enough information and time with him to effectively pretend…

Pretend they were in love. "And to business," she added, for herself as much as him. "Only."

CHAPTER SIX

THE glint of gold caught Finn's eye before he was fully awake. It took a second before he remembered why he had a ring on his left hand. And why he was waking up in a room he didn't recognize.

Last night. Marrying Ellie Winston. The rooftop dinner. The rings he'd given them—purchased earlier that evening by his assistant and delivered to the terrace before they arrived—so the two of them had the outward evidence of a marriage.

Then, after a dinner that alternated between tense and friendly, bringing her to her townhouse, and by mutual agreement, he'd spent the night. In the guest room.

Of his *wife's* home.

From outside the room, he heard the sound of music. Something upbeat…a current pop hit. He got out of bed, pulled on a pair of sweatpants from the bag he'd brought with him and padded out to the kitchen. Everything about Ellie's townhome was like her—clean, neat, bright. Lots of whites and yellows with accents of blue. It was the complete opposite of his heavy oak, dark carpet apartment. Softer, more feminine. Nice.

Ellie was standing at the kitchen sink, her hips swaying in time to the music as she filled a carafe with water. She was already dressed for work in a pale blue skirt and a short-sleeved white sweater. Her hair was curled, the tendrils curving over her shoulders and down her back in tantalizing spirals. Her feet were bare, and for some reason, that made him feel like he was intruding. It was such an unguarded, at-home kind of thing.

And oh, so intimate.

In the light of day, the reality of moving in with Ellie presented a bit of a dilemma. Like how he was going to resist her when she was right there every day, in bare feet, humming along to the radio. How was he going to pretend he hadn't felt anything with that kiss in the courthouse?

Because he did. He'd thought about it all last night, tossing and turning, a thousand percent aware she was also in bed, and mere feet down the hall. He'd made a concerted effort to keep their celebratory dinner more like a board meeting than a date, but still, a part of him had kept replaying that kiss. And had been craving another.

Hadn't he learned his lesson already? Getting distracted by a relationship left him vulnerable. Made him make mistakes, like nearly marrying someone who wanted only to destroy him. He saw where that kind of foolishness got a person—and it wasn't a path he wanted to travel.

So he forced his gaze away from her bare feet and her tantalizing curves, and cleared his throat. "Good morning."

She spun around, and nearly dropped the carafe. "Finn. Oh, hi. I almost forgot…" A flush filled her face. "Good morning. Do you want some coffee?"

"Yes. Please."

She busied herself with setting up the pot, then turning it on. When she was done, she pivoted back to him.

"I'm sorry I don't have much for breakfast. I'm usually running out the door with a muffin in my hand."

"A muffin's fine. Really. This whole...thing was un-expected." His gaze kept straying back to the ring on her hand. He was now the husband of Ellie Winston. No... Ellie McKenna.

Just a few days ago he'd been thinking how he wanted a relationship without any drama. One based solely on common interests, none of that silly romantic stuff that clouded his brain and muddled his thinking. Now, he had that—

And for some reason, it disappointed him like hell.

What was he thinking? He didn't need the crazy romantic notion of love. He needed something steady, dependable, as predictable as the columns in his general ledger. The problem was, there was a part of Ellie that Finn suspected, no, knew, was far from predictable. And that was dangerous.

The song shifted from pop to a ballad. The love song filled the room, stringing tension between them.

"I have, uh, blueberry and banana nut." She waved toward the breadbox. "Muffins, I mean."

He took a step farther into the kitchen. The walls were a butter-yellow, the cabinets a soft white. No clutter that he could see, merely a few things that added person-ality—a hand-painted ceramic bowl teeming with fruit, a deep green vase filled with fresh daisies, and a jade sculpture of a dragon, probably picked up in China. It seemed to suit her, this eclectic, homey mix.

Beside him, the coffeepot percolated with a steady drip-drip. The sun streamed in through the windows, showering those curls, those tantalizing curls, with gold. He wanted to reach up, capture one of those curls in his palm. "I'd love one."

"Which?"

It took him a second to realize she meant which flavor, not which he wanted—her or the muffins. "Blueberry, please."

"Sure." She pivoted away, fast. The breadbox door raised with a rattle. Ellie tugged out the plastic container holding the muffins, then spun back. The package tumbled out of her grasp and dropped to the floor. Muffins tumbled end over end and spun away, spinning a trail of crumbs. Ellie cursed.

Finn bent down, at the same time Ellie did, to reach for the runaway muffins. They knocked shoulders and Finn drew back. When had he become so clumsy? This wasn't his usual self. "Sorry."

"It's okay, it's my fault." She reached for the muffin closest to them, at the same time he did. Their hands brushed. She staggered to her feet, nearly toppling, and reached out a hand to steady herself. It connected with his bare chest, just a brief second, before she yanked her palm away.

A jolt of electricity ran through Finn. His gaze jerked to her face. Ellie's eyes were wide, her lips parted. "Sorry," he said again.

"No, I am." She looked away from him, back at the floor. "I can make toast, if you prefer."

Toast? Muffins? Had she been affected at all by that accidental touch? "I'm not hungry. I should get to work."

Yes, get to work, get to the office and get on with his day. Rather than indulge in any more of this craziness. Get his head clear—and back on straight.

"I'll clean this up," she said, gesturing to the mess on the floor. "If you want to hop in the shower and get ready."

"Sure, sure." He dumped the crumbs in his hand into the trash, then turned to go.

"Finn?"

His name rolled off her tongue, soft, easy. For a second, he wondered what it would be like to hear her say his name every day. Every morning. Every night. He turned back to face her, taking in those wide green eyes, the sweet smile that curved across her face, and yes, those bare feet. "Yeah?"

She shot him a grin. "Coffee's ready."

Coffee's ready.

A heavy blanket of disappointment hung over Finn while he got ready. Hell, what had he expected her to say? Stay? Kiss me? Take me back to the bedroom?

No, he didn't want that. He wanted exactly what he had—a platonic relationship that let him focus on work and didn't send his head, or his world, into a tailspin.

Except the image of Ellie in her kitchen, swaying to the music and doing something so mundane as making coffee, kept coming back to his mind. He had lived alone for too long, that was all. That was why the sight of her affected him so much.

He got ready, then headed out the door, leaving Ellie a note that he had to stop by his office and would meet her at WW later. He knew it was the coward's way out, but he'd been thrown by waking up in her place. It was all moving so fast, and he told himself he just needed some time to adjust.

Later that morning, he was heading up to the tenth floor of the building housing WW Architects, flanked by Noel and Barry, two of his best architects, who'd met him in the lobby. The team Finn brought in had been part of the bidding process, and was already familiar with the Piedmont hospital project, so the trio exchanged small talk until they reached Ellie's floor. A few minutes later, an assistant led them to a conference room where the WW staff had already assembled. Ellie stood at the head of the table. Her curly blond hair was now tucked into a tight bun, the bare feet were clad in sensible black pumps, and her curvy figure hidden beneath a jacket that turned the blue skirt into a suit.

She was all business now. Exactly what he wanted.

Then why did he feel a sense of loss?

"Thank you for coming today, gentlemen." Ellie made the introductions between her team and Finn's. Finn headed to the front of the room to stand beside Ellie. "Before we get started, we…I mean, Finn and I, have an announcement."

She exchanged a look with Finn. He nodded. They had talked about this last night, and decided the best way to spread the news was fast and first. "We…Ellie and I… we got *married*."

Jaws dropped. People stared.

"You got married?" Larry asked. "As in…married?"

"Last night." Ellie nodded and smiled, the kind of smile that reached deep into her eyes, lit up her features. Just like the smile of a happy new bride. "It was an impromptu thing."

"You married her?" Noel scowled at Finn. "Is *that* why we're working together?"

Finn wasn't about to tell their employees the real reason he had married Ellie. If he did, it would taint the project. No, let them all think it was some act of passion. Cover up the truth with a lie.

A lie that a part of Finn wished was true. The part that was still thinking about coffee with Ellie and seeing her in the kitchen. "Not at all. Working together is just a…fringe benefit," Finn said. "Ellie and I agreed to merge our companies for this project. After that, we go back to being separate entities."

Ellie leaned in and grabbed his arm. That same jolt of electricity rushed through his veins. "Separate business entities at least." She grinned up at him and for a half a second, he could almost believe she loved him. Damn, she was good at this.

"*You* eloped last night?" Noel let out a little a laugh. "I don't believe it. I'm sorry, Finn, but I just don't see you as the eloping kind."

Explaining that the practical, methodical Finn they all knew had done just that was suddenly much harder than he'd expected. "Well, I…I…"

"Blame it on me," Ellie said, pressing her head to his arm. "I didn't want the fanfare of a big event, and so I told Finn, let's just run to the courthouse and get it done. Then we can all get back to work." She peered up at him, her eyes soft and warm. "We'll take that honeymoon a little later."

"Uh…yeah," he said, his thoughts running rampant down the path of what a honeymoon with Ellie would be like. When she was looking at him like that, he could almost believe this was real. That at the end of the day, they were heading back to a little house in the suburbs with a fence and a dog and a dinner on the stove. And more—much, much more—after the dishes were done and the lights were dimmed. "We're, uh, planning on leaving as soon as this project is done."

"Well, then congratulations are in order," John said. He shook with Finn, then Ellic. "Best of luck to both of you." The rest of the group echoed John's sentiments. They congratulated, they shook and they beamed. And Ellie pulled the whole thing off with nary a blink.

"Okay, back to work. We have a major project ahead of us, and not a lot of time," Ellie said. "So as much as we'd love to take time for a celebration, we need to dive in and work until we have the particulars hammered out."

Larry, one of Ellie's architects, grumbled under his breath, but didn't voice any objections. The rest of the team seemed to be giving Finn's people the benefit of the doubt. "I appreciate you bringing us in on this project, Ellie," Finn said, rising to address the group. "I'm confident that by combining the experience of both McKenna Designs and WW Architectural Design, we can create a hospital that will outshine all others in the New England area."

Ellie shot him a smile. "That's our goal, too." She opened the folder before her. "Okay, let's get to work. Piedmont wants this design to be groundbreaking. One of the key elements that sold them on WW as the architects was our innovative approach. Rather than basing the design on existing models, WW talked about approaching the design process from the patient's perspective, from admission through discharge. The challenge is to create an environment that creates a healing atmosphere, one that offers warmth with minimal noise, while also keeping patient safety as the top priority."

"Excellent ideas," Finn said, nodding to Ellie.

"Thank you. Although I have to admit that one of the challenges we are having is creating that warm, healing atmosphere. WW specializes in corporate buildings, which aren't usually described as cozy." Ellie gestured toward Finn and his team. "I think if we combine our expertise in the safety arena, with yours in environment, we'll have a winner."

"I agree." Finn sketched out a drawing on the pad before him, then turned it toward Ellie and the others.

"We'll design standardized rooms, where every medical element is in the same place, no matter what floor or wing, yet also give each room its own flair. Install ambient lighting in addition to the harsher lighting needed for procedures, and soundproof the space so patients aren't bothered by constant pages and hallway traffic. Studies have shown that a warmer, quieter space speeds patient healing." Finn filled in another section of the drawing, sketching in fast movements, limited in details, focused on getting the bare bones on the page first. "We should also provide a small visiting area in each room for family members. Nothing huge, but something far superior in comfort and flexibility to the current models in today's hospitals."

"What about pricing? That kind of thing is going to raise the costs." Larry scowled. "Piedmont will not be happy."

"Easy," Finn said. "We call the vendors and tell them that they're going to be part of a groundbreaking new hospital. One that will have plenty of media coverage. They'll be jumping at the opportunity to be a part of that, and be very amenable to lowering their pricing."

"In other words, beat them up until they cave?" Larry said.

"I think it's a good strategy," Ellie said. "Thanks, Finn." She clapped her hands together and faced the room. "Okay, what else?"

As if a wall had been dismantled, the room erupted with ideas, people from both teams exchanging and brainstorming, no longer separated into an "us" and "them," but becoming one cohesive unit, brimming with creativity. Ellie got to her feet and jotted the ideas on the whiteboard behind her, quickly covering the wall-length space. Finn pulled out his computer to take notes, his fingers moving rapidly over the keys of his laptop. It occurred to him somewhere into the first hour that he and Ellie made a good team. Neither tried to outtalk the other or prove their idea the best. Their thoughts seemed to merge, with her suggesting one thought, and him finishing it. He was so used to being the one in charge, the one who had to pull the team together and take the lead, that suddenly sharing the job was…nice. When the group broke for lunch, Finn stayed behind in the room.

"We work well together," he said, rising and crossing to Ellie. He picked up a second eraser and helped her clean off the whiteboard.

She smiled. "We do indeed."

Out in the hall, the team was whispering and exchanging glances in the direction of the conference room. "Seems we've got people talking," Finn said.

"It was bound to happen. Though I thought we'd have a little more time to…"

"Work out our story?"

"Yeah. We should have talked about it more last night. I really didn't think that part through."

"Me, either. I was too focused on work."

She laughed. "I know what you mean. That's how my days have been, too." She moved away from him, then stretched, working out the kinks in her back. He was tempted to offer her a massage, but instead he kept his hands at his side. A massage was definitely not part of this…partnership.

"You pulled it off well," Finn said. "Hell, even I believed…"

She cocked her head. "Believed what?"

"That you were wildly in love with me."

She laughed, and that told him that there was no doubt she'd been acting earlier. Finn told himself he was glad.

"Well, I'm glad it worked. Anyway, I guess I'll see you back here in a little while."

"Wait. Do you have lunch plans?" he asked, then wondered what he was doing. Was he asking her on a date—a date with his wife—or a simple lunch meeting to discuss the project? He told himself it was just because people would expect them to eat together. He was keeping up the facade, nothing more.

"I have one of those frozen dinners in the office refrigerator." She gave him an apologetic smile. "I usually eat at my desk."

"So do I." Outside the sun shone bright and hazy, a warm day with the promising scent of spring in the air. Inside, all they had was climate controlled air and a sterile office environment. The same kind of place where he spent five, sometimes six, days a week. He thought of the calls waiting to be returned, the emails waiting to be answered, the projects waiting to be completed. Then he looked at Ellie, and wanted only a few minutes with her, just long enough to hear her laugh again, see her smile. Then he'd be ready to go back to the To Do lists and other people's expectations. "Let's go have lunch on the plaza. Get out of here for a while. I think both of us have spent far too many afternoons at our desks."

"Two days in a row, taking time off? My, my, Finn, whatever will people say?"

Damn. He was really starting to like the way she said his name. "Oh, I think we've already given them plenty to talk about, don't you?"

She looked up at him, and a smile burst across her face. It sent a rush through Finn, and he decided that if he did nothing else, he would make Ellie smile again. And again.

"Oh my, yes, I do believe we've done that in spades,

Mr. McKenna." Then her green eyes lit with a tease and she put her hand in his. "What's a little more?"

As time ticked by and the afternoon sun made a slow march across the sky, Ellie was less and less able to concentrate on her sandwich or anything Finn was saying. On her way into work that morning, Ellie had called Linda and left her a message telling her that she had gotten married, and now the wait for Linda's return call seemed agonizing. Thank God for the meeting, which had taken her mind off the wait, and for Finn, who had convinced her to leave the office and get some fresh air. Still, she had checked her cell at least a dozen times.

Finn had taken two calls, and she'd been impressed with the way he handled business. Efficiently, with barely a wasted word. He argued with a contractor who wanted to make a change that Finn felt would compromise the building's structure, and negotiated a lower price on materials for another project.

"I can see where you got the nickname," Ellie said when Finn hung up. "You're relentless."

"I just like to get the job done."

"Yeah, but negotiating a discount, while at the same time moving up the deadline, I'd say you pulled off a miracle."

"Just doing my job." He seemed embarrassed by her attention.

"You do it well. Does that come from being the oldest?"

"I don't know. I guess I never thought about that. Maybe it does."

"Well, it seems to be working for you." She felt her phone buzz and checked the screen, then tucked it away.

"Waiting on a call yourself?"

She nodded. "From the agency. I told my adoption co-ordinator that we got married. I'm just waiting to hear back."

He unwrapped the sandwich they had bought from a street vendor, but didn't take a bite. "How are you planning on doing this?"

"Doing what? The interview? It should be relatively straightforward."

"No, not that. This whole—" he made a circle with the sandwich "—raising a child alone thing."

"People do it every day."

"Not people who also happen to be CEOs of busy, growing companies."

"True." She glanced at the park across the street. It bustled with activity. Children ran to and fro, filling the small park with the sound of laughter. Dogs chased Frisbees and couples picnicked on the grass. "I'm sure it's going to be hard." That was an understatement. She'd worried constantly that she wouldn't be able to juggle it all. "But I'll figure it out somehow."

"Would it have been better if you had waited to marry someone who could…well, create a real family with you?" Finn asked.

Ellie watched a family of three pass by them, mother and father on either side of a toddler, who held both his parent's hands and danced between them. "Maybe. But honestly, I never intended to get married."

"Ever?"

"I guess I was always afraid to get married," Ellie said softly.

"Afraid? Of what?"

"Of being a disappointment and of getting my children caught in an endless limbo of…dissatisfaction." Ellie sighed. "I looked at my parents, and they were more roommates than spouses. They came and went on their own schedules, and we very rarely did anything as a family. I guess I never felt like I knew how to do it better."

"I think a lot of people feel that way," Finn said after a moment.

"Do you?"

He let out a short laugh. "When did this become about me?"

"I'm just curious. You seem the kind of man who would want to settle down. Complete that life list or whatever."

"Yeah, well, I'm not." He got to his feet and tossed the remains of his sandwich in the trash.

He had shut the door between them. She had opened herself to him, and he had refused to do the same. The distance stung.

Ellie glanced at the family across the park. They had stopped walking and were sitting on the grass, sharing a package of cookies. The mother teased the son with a cookie that she placed in his palm, then yanked back, making him giggle. Over and over again they played that game, and the little boy's laughter rang like church bells.

A bone-deep ache ran through her. Deep down inside, yes, she did want that, did crave those moments, that togetherness. She'd always thought she didn't, but she'd been lying to herself. ·

She watched Finn return to the bench and realized she wasn't going to find that fairy tale with the Hawk. He was going about their marriage like he did any other business deal—with no emotion and no personal ties.

It was what she had wanted. But now that she had it, victory tasted stale.

Because a part of her had already started to get very, very used to him being her husband.

CHAPTER SEVEN

AN HOUR on the treadmill. A half hour with the weight machines. And a hell of a sweat.

But it wasn't enough. No matter how much time Finn spent in the gym, tension still knotted his shoulders, frustration still held tight to his chest. He'd been unable to forget Ellie—or bring himself to go home to her.

Home. To his wife.

Already he was getting far too wrapped up in her, he'd realized. They'd had that conversation at lunch about marriage, and he had found himself wanting to tell her that he felt the same way. That he had never imagined himself getting married, either.

Then he had come to his senses before he laid his heart bare again, and made the same mistakes he'd made before. He'd watched his parents locked in an emotional roller coaster of love and hate, then repeated those mistakes at the end of his relationship with Lucy. No way was he going to risk that again with Ellie. She saw him as a means to an end—a father on paper for her child— and nothing more.

He pulled on the lat bar, leaning back slightly on the padded bench, hauling the weights down. His shoulders protested, his biceps screamed, but Finn did another rep. Another. Over and over, he tugged the heavy weight down.

It wasn't just the distraction of getting close to Ellie that had him sweating it out in the gym. It was the growing reality of the child she was about to adopt.

No, that *they* were about to adopt. He'd promised Ellie that he would go along with her plan, but now he was wondering if that was the right thing to do.

How could he be a temporary husband, temporary dad, and then, at the end of the hospital project, just pack up his things and go? If anyone knew firsthand what losing a parent suddenly could do to a child, it was Finn. He'd gone through it himself, and watched the impact on his younger brothers. They'd been cast adrift, emotional wrecks who took years to heal, even with the loving arms of their grandparents. How could he knowingly do that to a child?

He gave the lat bar another pull, his muscles groaning in protest, then lowered the weight back to the base. He was finished with his workout, but no closer to any of the answers he needed.

He showered, got dressed in jeans and a T-shirt, then hailed a cab and headed across town toward Ellie's townhouse. Night had begun to fall, draping purple light over the city of Boston. It was beautiful, the kind of clear, slightly warm night that would be perfect for a walk. Except Finn never took time to do that. He wondered for a moment what his life would be like if he was the kind of man who did.

If he was the kind of man who had a real marriage, and spent his life with someone who wanted to stroll down the city streets as dusk was falling and appreciate the twinkling magic. But he wasn't. And he was foolish to believe in a fantasy life. His mother had been like that—full of romantic notions that burned out when she saw the reality of her unhappy marriage. Finn was going to be clearheaded about his relationships. No banking on superfluous things like starry skies and red roses.

He paid the cabbie, then headed up the stairs to Ellie's building. He paused at the door and caught her name on the intercom box. Ellie Winston.

His wife.

Already, he knew they had a connection. It wasn't friendship, but something more, something indefinable. A hundred times during the meeting today, he found his mind wandering, his gaze drifting to her. He wondered a hundred things about her—what her favorite color was, if she preferred spring or fall, if she slept on the left side of the bed or the right. Even as he told himself to pull back, to not get any deeper connected to this woman than he already was. This was a business arrangement.

Nothing more.

As he headed inside, he marveled again at the building she had chosen—the complete opposite to the modern glass high-rise that housed his apartment. Ellie lived in one of Boston's many converted brownstones. Ellie's building sported a neat brick facade and window boxes filled with pansies doing a tentative wave to spring adorned every window. The building's lobby featured a white tile floor and thick, dark woodwork. The staircase was flanked by a curved banister on one side, a white plaster wall on the other. A bank of mailboxes were stationed against one wall, lit from above by a black wrought-iron light fixture that looked older than Finn's grandmother, but had a certain Old World charm.

He liked this place. A lot. It had a…homey feeling. At the same time, he cautioned himself not to get too comfortable. They weren't making this a permanent thing, and letting himself feel at home would be a mistake. He'd get used to it, and begin to believe this was something that it wasn't. He'd fooled himself like that once before.

Never again.

He found Ellie in the kitchen again, rinsing some dishes and loading them into the dishwasher. "Hi."

Kind of a lame opening but what did one say to a wife who wasn't a real wife?

She turned around. "Hi yourself. I'm sorry, I ate without you. I wasn't sure what your plan…" She put up her hands. "Well, you certainly don't have to answer to me. It's not like we're really married or anything."

There. The truth of it.

"I grabbed a bite to eat after the gym." He dropped his gym bag on the floor, then hung his dry cleaning over the chair. "Did you find out when the interview would be?"

"In a couple days. Linda's trying to coordinate all the schedules."

"Okay. Good." The sooner the interview was over, the sooner they could go their separate ways. And that was what he wanted, wasn't it?

"After this morning, I think we should work on our story," she said. "You know, in case they ask us a lot of questions. I don't want it to seem like…"

"We barely know each other."

She nodded. "Yes." She gestured toward a door at the back. "We can sit on the balcony out back if you want. It's not a rooftop terrace, but we'll be able to enjoy the evening a little."

They got drinks—red wine for him, iced tea for her— and Ellie assembled a little platter of cheese and crackers. Finn would have never thought of a snack, or if he had, it probably would have been something salty, served straight from the bag. But Ellie laid everything out on a long red platter, and even included napkins. The night air drifted over them, lazy and warm. "You thought of everything,"

She shrugged. "Nothing special. And it's not quite the evening you planned."

"No, it's not." He picked up a cracker and a piece of cheese, and devoured them in one bite. "It's better."

She laughed. "How is that? There's no musicians, no twinkling lights, no five-course meal. It's just crackers and cheese on the balcony."

"Done by you. Not by others. I don't have that home-making touch. At all."

"I'm not exactly Betty Crocker myself. But I can assemble a hell of a crudités platter." She laughed again. "So I take it you can't cook?"

"Not so much as a scrambled egg. But I can order takeout like a pro. My grandmother is the real chef in the family. She doesn't cook much now, but when I was a kid, she did everything from scratch."

Ellie picked up her glass and took a sip of tea. "Where are you parents? Do they live in Boston?"

The question was an easy one, the kind people asked each other all the time. But for some reason, this time, it hit Finn hard and he had to take a minute to compose the answer.

"No. They don't. Not anymore." Finn was quiet for a moment. "My parents…died in a car accident, when I was eleven. Brody was eight, Riley was just six."

"Oh, Finn, I'm so sorry." She reached for him, and laid a soft hand on top of his arm. It was a simple, comforting touch, but it seemed to warm Finn to his core. He wanted to lean into that touch, to let it warm the icy spots in his heart.

But he didn't.

"We went and lived with my grandparents," he continued. "I think us three boys drove my grandmother nuts with all our noise and fighting."

"I bet you three were a handful."

He chuckled. "She called us a basketful of trouble, but she loved us. My grandmother was a stern, strict parent, but one who would surprise us at the oddest times with a new toy or a bunch of cookies."

Ellie smiled. "She sounds wonderful."

"She is. I think every kid needs a grandmother like that. One time, Brody and I were arguing over a toy. I can't remember what toy it was or why. So my grandmother made us rake two ends of the yard, working toward each other. By the time we met in the middle, we had this massive pile of leaves. So we jumped in them. And the fight was forgotten."

Ellie laughed. "Sounds like you learned some of your art of compromise from her."

"Yeah, I guess I did. She taught me a lot." He hadn't shared that much of his personal life with anyone in a long, long time. Even Lucy hadn't known much about him. They'd mainly talked about work when they were together.

Was that because she didn't care, or because it was easier? Or was it because Finn had always reserved a corner of himself from Lucy, with some instinctual self-preservation because he knew there was something amiss in their relationship?

Was Ellie's interest real, or was she just gathering facts for the interview? And why did he care? On his way here from the gym, he had vowed to keep this impersonal, business only. Why did he keep treading into personal waters? He knew better, damn it.

"I think every person needs someone like your grandmother in their lives," Ellie said softly.

"Yeah," he said. "They do."

Damn, it was getting warm out here. He glanced over at Ellie to find her watching him. She opened her mouth, as if she was going to ask another question, to get him to open up more, but he cut her off by reaching into his pocket for a sheet of paper. He handed it to her. "I, uh, thought you'd want to know some things about me for the interview. So I wrote them down."

She read over the sheet. "Shoe size. Suit jacket size. Car model." Then she looked up at him. "This doesn't tell me anything about you, except maybe what to get you for Christmas."

"That's all the particulars you would need right there."

She dropped the sheet of paper onto a nearby table, then drew her knees up to her chest and wrapped her arms around her legs. She'd changed into sweatpants and a soft pink T-shirt after work, and she looked as comfortable as a pile of pillows. "What a wife should know about a husband isn't on that list, Finn."

"Well, of course it is. A wife would know my shoe size and my car—"

"No, no. A wife would know your heart. She'd know what made you who you are. What your dreams are, your fears, your pet peeves. She'd be able to answer any question about you because she knows you as well as she knows herself."

He shifted in his chair. The cracker felt heavy in his stomach. "No one knows me like that."

"Why?"

It was such a simple question, just one word, but that didn't mean Finn had an answer. "I don't know."

"Well, surely the woman you were engaged to got

to know you like that. Like the story about your grand-mother. That's what I want to hear more of. Or tell me about your fiancée. Why did you two not work out?"

"I don't want to talk about Lucy."

Ellie let out a gust. "Finn, you have to talk about something. We're supposed to know each other inside and out."

"That's why I gave you the list—"

"The list doesn't tell me anything more about you than I already knew from reading the magazine article." She let out a gust and got to her feet. For a while she stood at the railing, looking out over the darkened homes. Then she turned back to face him. "Why won't you get close to me?" Her voice was soft and hesitant. It was the kind of sound that Finn wished he could curl into. "You take two steps forward, then three back. Why?"

"I don't do that." He rose and turned to the other end of the balcony, watching a neighbor taking his trash to the curb. It was all so mundane, so much of what a home should be like. Between the crackers and the cheese and the sweatpants—

Damn, it was like a real marriage.

"What are we doing here, Finn?" Ellie asked, coming around to stand beside him.

When she did, he caught the scent of her perfume. The same dark jasmine, with vanilla tones dancing just beneath the floral fragrance. It was a scent he'd already memorized, and every time he caught a whiff of those tantalizing notes, he remembered the first time he'd been close enough to smell her perfume.

He'd been kissing her. Sealing their marriage vows in Charlie's office. And right now, all he could think about was kissing her again. And more, much more.

Damn.

"We're pretending to be married," he said.

"Are we?" He didn't respond. She lifted her gaze to his. "Can I ask you something?"

"Sure."

She let a beat pass. Another. Still her emerald gaze held his. "Why did you agree to marry me?"

"Because you said that's what it would take. To get on board with the hospital project."

"You are 'the Hawk,' Finn McKenna," she said, putting air quotes around his nickname. "You could negotiate your way out of an underground prison. But when I proposed this…marriage, you didn't try to negotiate at all. You agreed. What I want to know is why."

The night air seemed to still. Even the whoosh-whoosh of traffic seemed to stop. Nothing seemed to move or breathe in the space of time that Ellie waited for his answer. He inhaled, and that damned jasmine perfume teased at his senses, reawakened his desire.

Why had he married her? She was right—he could have offered something else in return for her cooperation on the hospital project. Or he could have just said no. "I guess I just really needed that project to help my business get back on track."

She took a step closer, and lifted her chin. "I don't believe you."

"Truly, it was all about business for me."

"And that was all?"

She was mere inches away from him. A half step, no more, and she'd be against him. Desire pulsed in his veins, thundered in his head. His gaze dropped from her eyes to her lips, to her curves. "No," he said, with a ragged breath, cursing the truth that slipped through his lips. "It's not."

Then he closed that gap, and reached up to capture

one of those tendrils of her hair. All day, he'd wanted to do this, to let one silky strand slip through his grasp. "Is it for you?" he asked.

She swallowed, then shook her head. "No. It's not." She bit her lip, let it go. "It's becoming more for me. A lot more."

Finn watched her lips form the words, felt the whisper of her breath against his mouth. And he stopped listening to his common sense.

He leaned in, and kissed Ellie. She seemed to melt into him, her body curving against his, fitting perfectly against his chest, in his arms. She was soft where he was hard, sweet where he was sour, and the opposite of him in every way. Finn kissed her slow at first, then harder, faster, letting the raging need sweep over him and guide his mouth, his hands. She pressed into him, and he groaned, in agony for more of her, of this.

His cell phone began to ring, its insistent trill ripping through the fog in Finn's brain. He jerked away from Ellie, then stepped away. "I'm sorry." He flipped out the phone, but the call had already gone to voice mail. The interruption had served its purpose.

Finn had regained his senses.

Ellie stepped toward him, a smile on her lips, and everything in Finn wanted to take her in his arms and pick up where they left off. But doing so would only do the one thing he was trying to avoid—

Plunge him headlong down that path of wild and crazy. The kind of roller-coaster romance that led to bad decisions, bad matches, and in the end, unhappiness and broken hearts.

"We can't do this." He put some distance between them and picked up his glass, just to have something to do with his hands—something other than touch Ellie again.

"Can't do what?" A smile curved across her face. "Let this lead to something more than a contract?"

"Especially not that. We can't treat this like...like a real marriage. It's a business partnership. And that's all." He shook his head and put the glass back on the tray. The remains of their snack sat there, mocking him. Tempting him to go back to pretending this was something that it wasn't.

But Ellie wasn't so easily dissuaded. She stood before him, hands on her hips. "What are you so afraid of?"

"I'm not afraid of anything. I just think it's best if we keep this business only."

"So that's what that kiss was, business only?"

"No, that was a mistake. One I won't make again."

"And the rooftop dinner? The kiss in the courthouse? Also mistakes?"

He sighed. This was why he hadn't wanted to go down this path. He could already see hurt brimming in Ellie's eyes. He'd done this—he'd made her believe their fake marriage might be leading to something more—and he'd been wrong.

Was any project worth hurting Ellie? Seeing her crying, just like he had seen his mother crying so many times?

He exhaled, then pushed the words out. The words he should have said long ago. "After the interview, I don't think we should wait to annul this marriage." There. He'd said it. Fast, like ripping off a bandage.

Didn't stop it from hurting, though.

Her green eyes filled with disbelief. A ripple of shock filled her features. "What?"

"The business deal can be maintained if you want,"

he said. He kept his voice neutral, his stance profes-sional. If he treated this like business as usual, perhaps she would, too. But the notes of her perfume kept teas-ing at his senses while the tears in her green eyes begged him to reconsider. Finn struggled to stick to his resolve. This was the best thing, all around. "Uh, if you like, I'll keep my team in place at WW, and help you through the project. It seems like they're working well together. No reason to break that up."

"That wasn't the deal. You were supposed to help me adopt Jiao."

"I'll do my part. When the interview is set up, just let me know and I'll be here for that."

"Pretending to be my husband."

"Wasn't that the arrangement?"

She didn't say anything for a while. Outside her build-ing, a car honked, and a dog barked. Night birds twit-tered at each other, and the breeze whispered over them all.

"Was that all you were doing a minute ago? Sealing a business deal?"

She made him sound so cold, calculated. So like the Hawk nickname he hated. "You think that's the only reason I kissed you?"

"Isn't it? You wanted an alliance that would help your company. I wanted a child. We each get what we want out of this marriage. It's as simple as that. That's all this marriage is about. A simple business transaction." She took a step closer, her gaze locked on his. "Isn't it? Or did it start to become something more for you, too?"

She was asking him for the truth. Why had he mar-ried her if it wasn't about the business?

He couldn't tell her it was because he was tired of sleeping on that sofa bed. That he was tired of hearing nothing other than his own breath in his apartment. Tired of spending his days working and his nights wondering why he was working so hard. And that when he had met Ellie he had started to wonder what it would be like to have more.

But he didn't.

Because doing that would open a window into his heart, and if he did that, he'd never be able to walk away from Ellie Winston. He'd get tangled up in the kind of heated love story that he had always done his best to avoid. No, better to keep this cold, impersonal. Let her think the worst of him.

He let out a gust. "This is anything but simple."

"Why? What is so bad about getting involved with someone, Finn? What makes you so afraid of doing that?"

"I'm not afraid of getting involved. We got married, remember?"

"In name only. That's not a relationship. It's a contract. And I know that's what I said I wanted when we started this thing, but…" She let out a long breath and shook her head. "You know, a few times, I've thought I've seen a different side of you, a side that is downright human. And that made me wonder what it would be like to take a chance with you. I'm not a woman who takes chances easily, especially with my heart. But in the end, you keep coming back to being the Hawk."

He scowled. "That's not true."

"You're a coward, Finn." She turned away. "I don't know why I thought…why I thought anything at all."

Why couldn't she understand that he was trying to be smart, to put reality ahead of a fantasy they would never have? Acting without thinking and living in a dream bubble got people hurt. Ellie needed to understand that.

"You think we can turn this fantasy into a real marriage?" he asked. "Tell me the truth, Ellie. Was a part of you hoping that maybe, just maybe, we'd work out and make a happy little family with two-point-five kids and a dog?"

"No." She shook her head, and tears brimmed in her eyes. Above them, a light rain began to fall, but they both ignored it. "Not anymore."

His gaze went to the glass balcony door. The reflection of the neighborhood lights shimmered on the glass like mischievous eyes. Droplets of rain slid slowly down the glass, and Finn thought how like tears the rain could appear. "I'm sorry," he said. "But I have to be clear. I can't give you any more than what the contract stipulated."

Ellie didn't see the ramifications that he could. He had been through this already, seen his parents suffer every day they lived together. Sure, he and Ellie could have some hot, fiery romance, but in the end, they'd crash and burn, and the child would be the one who suffered the most. She was already starting to head down that road, and if he didn't detour them now, it would go nowhere good.

Tears began to slide down Ellie's cheeks, and for a moment, Finn's determination faltered. "That's all I am? A contract?"

"That's what you wanted, Ellie. And it's what's best for all of us." Then he turned on his heel and headed out into the rain.

Before the tears in her eyes undid all his resolve.

CHAPTER EIGHT

HE WAS having a good day. The smile on Henry Winston's face told Ellie that, along with the doctor's tentatively positive report. They were on an upswing right now, and her father was gaining ground. For the first time, the doctor had used the words "when he goes home."

Gratitude flooded Ellie, and she scooted the vinyl armchair closer to her father's bedside. Happy sunlight streamed through the windows of his room at Brigham and Women's Hospital. Her father had more color in his face today. The tray of food beside him was nearly empty. All good signs. Very good.

After last night's bitter disappointment with Finn, Ellie could use some good news. She'd tossed and turned all night, trying to think of a way to convince Finn to help her with Jiao. If he didn't, how would she make this work? He hadn't said for sure he'd get an annulment, but she hadn't heard from him since the conversation on the balcony. She could pick up the phone and call him herself, but she didn't. Because she didn't want to hear him say he'd ended their marriage. And ended Ellie's hopes for adopting Jiao.

Maybe Linda could try appealing to the Chinese again. Perhaps if they saw how committed Ellie was to adopting Jiao, they'd relent on the marriage rule.

Ellie bit back a sigh. From all Linda had told her, that was highly unlikely. Ellie was back at square one, with Jiao stuck in the same spot. Finn had let her down. He'd accused her of wanting this to be a real marriage.

Was he right? Did a part of her hope, after those kisses and that dinner, and all the jokes and smiles, that maybe this was turning into something more than just a platonic partnership?

She glanced out the window, at the city that held them both, and at the same time separated them, and realized yes, she had. She'd let herself believe in the fairy tale. She'd started to fall for him, to let down her guard, to do the one thing she'd vowed she wouldn't do—entangle her heart.

Time to get real, she told herself, and stop seeing happy endings where there weren't any.

For now, Ellie focused on her father instead. One thing at a time. "How are you doing, Dad?"

"Much better now that you're here." He gave her a smile, one that was weaker than Henry's usual hearty grin. But beneath the thick white hair, the same green eyes as always lit with happiness at her presence. "They've got me on a new med. So far, it seems to be working pretty well." He lifted an arm, did a weak flex. "I'll be ready to run the Boston marathon before you know it."

She laughed. "And the Ironman after that?"

"Of course." He grinned, then flicked off his bedside television. His roommate had gone home yesterday, so the hospital room was quiet—or as quiet as a room in one of Boston's busiest medical facilities could be. "How are you doing, Ellie girl?"

"I'm fine, Dad. You don't need to worry about me."

"Ah, but I do. There's some things that don't stop just because your kids grow up."

She gave her father's hand a tight squeeze. She wasn't about to unload her problems on his shoulders. He had much more important things to worry about. "You just concentrate on getting better."

"How are things going with the adoption? I'd sure love to meet my granddaughter."

Ellie sighed. "I've run into a bit of a snag." Then she forced a smile to her face. Worrying her father—about anything—was not what she wanted. Henry didn't need to know about her marriage or her new husband's refusal to help. Chances were, Finn had already filed the annulment and Ellie's marriage was over before it began. For the hundredth time, she was glad she'd kept the elopement a secret from her father. "It'll be fine. It'll just take a little bit longer to bring Jiao home."

"You sure? Do you want me to call someone? Hire a lawyer?" Her father started to reach for the bedside phone, but Ellie stopped him.

"It'll be fine. I swear. Don't worry about it at all." She didn't know any of that for sure, particularly after Finn had told her he wanted nothing to do with the adoption, but she wasn't about to involve her poor sick father. "Just a tiny delay. Nothing more."

"Well, good. I can't wait to meet her. I've seen enough pictures and heard enough about her that I feel like I know her already." Her father settled back against the pillows on his bed, his face wan and drawn. "Hand me that water, will you, honey?"

"Sure, sure, Dad." She got her father's water container, and spun the straw until it faced Henry. She helped him take it, and bring it to his mouth, then sat back. "You sure you're up to a visit?"

He put down the water, then gave her a smile. "Seeing my little girl always makes me feel better. Now, talk to me about something besides doctors and medications. Tell me how things are at the company."

"Good." She hadn't told her father about any of the problems she'd encountered with Farnsworth quitting and the rush to get the Piedmont project underway. She wasn't about to start now. Maybe down the road when he was stronger and feeling better.

He tsk-tsked her. "You always tell me that things are good. I know you're lying." He covered her hand with his own. "I know you have the best of intentions, but really, you can talk to me. Use me as a sounding board."

Oh, how she wished she could. But the doctor had been firm—no unnecessary stress or worries. Her father, who had worked all his adult life, had a lot of trouble distancing himself from the job, and right now, that was what he needed most to do. Whatever she wanted—or needed—could wait. "You need to concentrate on getting better, Dad, not on what is happening at work."

"All I do is lie here and concentrate on getting better." He let out a sigh. Frustration filled his green eyes, and knitted his brows. "This place is like prison. Complete with the crappy food. I need more to do. Something to challenge me."

"I brought you a lot of books. And there are magazines on the counter. A TV right here. If you want something else to read—"

He waved all of that off. "Talk to me about work."

"Dad—"

He leaned forward. The strong, determined Henry Winston she knew lit his features. "I love you, Ellie, and I love you for being so protective of me. But talking about work *keeps* me from worrying about work. I'm not worried about you being in charge—you're capable and smart, and I know you want that business to succeed as much as I do—but I miss being plugged in, connected. That company is as much a part of me as my right arm."

She sighed. She knew her father. He had the tenacity of a bulldog, and now that he was feeling better, she doubted she could put him off much longer about WW Architectural Design. Maybe she could set his mind at ease by sharing a small amount of information, and that would satisfy his workaholic tendencies. "Okay, but if your blood pressure so much as blips, we're talking only about gardening the rest of the day."

He grimaced at his least favorite topic, then crossed his heart. "I promise."

"Okay." She sat back and filled him in, starting with a brief recap of Farnsworth's defection, followed by glossing over most of the setbacks on the Piedmont project, and finally, touting the positive aspects of her temporary alliance with Finn. She kept the news mostly upbeat, and left out all mentions of her elopement.

"You are working with Finn McKenna," Henry said. It was a statement, not a question.

She nodded. "He has the experience we need. I could hire a new architect but we don't have enough time to do another candidate search and then bring that person up to speed. The prelims are due the fifteenth."

"Finn McKenna, though? That man is not one you should easily trust. He's made an art form out of taking over small companies like ours. You know he's our competition, right?"

"Yes, and we have worked out an amicable and fair arrangement. His business got into a little trouble—"

"Do you know what that trouble was? Did he tell you?"

"He didn't give me specifics." Dread sank in Ellie's gut. She could hear the message in her father's tone. There was something she had missed, something she had overlooked. Damn. She had been too distracted to probe Finn, to push him to tell her more.

She knew better. She'd rushed headlong into an alliance because her mind was on saving Jiao and nothing else.

"He got involved with the daughter of a competitor. In fact, I think he was engaged to her," Henry said. "And when things went south in the relationship, several of his clients defected to the other firm, taking all their business with them. I heard Finn raised a ruckus over at his office, but it was too late. A lot of people said he only proposed to her so he could take over her company and when it ended badly, she stole his clients instead."

Daughter of a competitor. Wasn't that what she was, too? Had Finn married her for control of the company?

Oh, God, had she made a deal with the devil? Her gut told her no, that Finn was not the cutthroat businessman depicted by the media. But how well did she really know him? Every time she tried to get close to him, he shut the door.

Wasn't this exactly why she had stayed away from marriage all these years? She'd seen how her parents had been virtual strangers, roommates sharing a roof. She didn't want to end up the same way, married to someone she hardly knew because she mistook infatuation for something real.

Ironic how that had turned out. Well, either way, the marriage would be over soon. She told herself it was better that way for all of them.

"Just be cautious, honey," Henry said. "I've heard Finn is ruthless. You know they call him—"

"The Hawk." The nickname had seemed like a joke before, but now it struck a chord. Had she missed the point? Was this entire marriage a plan by Finn to get his company back—

By taking over WW Architectural Design?

Maybe his "help" was all about helping his own bottom line. "I'm sure Finn will be fine," she said, more to allay her own fears than her father's. Because all of a sudden she wasn't so sure anything was going to be fine. "He's really smart and has been a great asset on this project."

"I'd just be very cautious about an alliance with him," her father said. "He's one of those guys who's always out to win. No matter the cost."

"He's been very up-front with me, Dad. I don't think he has a hidden agenda." Though could she say that for a hundred percent? Just because she'd married Finn and kissed him didn't mean she knew much more than she had two days ago. Every time she tried to get close to him, he pushed her away.

"Don't trust him, that's all I'm saying. He's backed into a corner, and a dog that's in a corner will do anything to get out."

Anything. Like marry a total stranger.

And try to steal her father's legacy right out from under her.

CHAPTER NINE

RILEY and Brody dragged Finn out for breakfast. The two brothers showed up at Finn's office, and refused to take no for an answer.

"Why are you stuck in this stuffy office, instead of spending time with your hot new wife?" Riley said. "You've been married for almost a week now, and I swear, you spend even more time here than you did before you got married."

Brody gave Riley's words a hearty hear-hear. "Jeez, Finn. You'd think being married would change you."

He didn't want his brothers reminding him about his marriage—or lack of one. Or the fact that he hadn't seen Ellie in a couple of days. He'd gone home after that night on the balcony, and had yet to return to her apartment, or her office.

He'd sent his senior architects to most of the meetings at WW, and only gone to one when Ellie wasn't scheduled to be there. He conferred with his team back here at his office, and in general, avoided Ellie. Entirely. He used the excuse that the drawings were due in a few days, but really, he knew that was all it was—an excuse. An excuse to keep his distance. Because every time he was with her, he considered the kind of heady relationship he'd spent a lifetime avoiding. "I am changed."

Riley arched a brow. Brody outright laughed. "Sure you are. Prove it and leave the shackles behind for a little while."

Finn scowled. "I have work to do."

"Come on, let's get something to eat," Brody said. Like the other McKenna boys, Brody had dark brown hair, blue eyes and a contagious smile. As the middle brother, he had a mix of both their personalities—a little serious and at the same time a little mischievous.

Riley turned to Brody. "What do you say we kidnap him?"

Brody put a finger on his chin and feigned deep thought. "I don't know. He's pretty stubborn."

"We'll just tie him up." Riley grinned. "So there's your choice, Finn. Either come with us or we're going to haul you out of here like an Oriental rug."

Finn chuckled. "Okay. I can see when I've been beaten." He wagged a finger at them. "But I only have time for a cup of coffee, no more."

The three of them headed out of the office, and instead of going down Beacon to their usual haunt, Riley took a right and led them toward a small corner diner on a busy street. The sign over the bright white and yellow awning read Morning Glory Diner. It looked cheery, homey. The opposite of the kind of place the McKenna boys usually frequented. "Hey, I really don't have room in my schedule to go all over the city for some coffee," Finn said. "My day is very—"

Riley put a hand on his arm. "You gotta ask yourself, what do you have room for?"

"Because it's sure not sex." Brody laughed. "I can't believe you've been at work bright and early every morning. Haven't you heard of a honeymoon period?"

Finn wasn't about to tell his brothers that his was far

from a conventional marriage. A honeymoon was not part of the deal. Nor was he even living with his "wife."

"Take advice on marriage from you? The eternal bachelor twins?"

"Hey, I may not be interested in getting married— ever." Riley chuckled. "But even I know a newly married man should be spending all his time with his new bride."

"Yeah, and in bed," Brody added.

Damn. Just the words *bed* and *wife* had Finn's mind rocketing down a path that pictured Ellie's luscious curves beneath him, her smile welcoming him into her heart, her bed, and then tasting her skin. Taking his time to linger in all the hills and valleys, tasting every inch of her before making slow, hot love to her. Again and again.

He'd had that dream a hundred times in the days since he'd met her. He found himself thinking of her at the end of his day, the beginning of his day, and nearly every damned minute in between.

And that alone was reason enough to end this. He was a practical man, one who made sensible decisions. The sensible side of him said keeping his distance from Ellie was the wisest course. The one that would head off the disaster he'd created before. A part of him was relieved.

Another part was disappointed.

The part that dreamed about Ellie Winston and wondered what it would be like to consummate their temporary marital union.

Finn cleared his throat and refocused. He was in a platonic marriage, and there was no definition of that word that included having sex. "I'm not taking relationship advice from you two."

"Maybe you should, brother." Riley quirked a brow at him, as they entered the diner and sidled up to the counter. The diner's namesake of bright blue flowers decorated the border of the room, and offset the bright yellow and white color scheme. "So, besides the fact that you aren't in bed with her right now, how is it going with the new missus?"

"Do you want to talk about anything else this morning?"

Riley glanced at Brody. "Not me. You?"

"Nope. Finn's life is my number-one topic of conversation."

He loved his brothers but sometimes they took wellmeaning just a step—or ten—too far. "Well then, you two will be talking to yourselves." Finn ordered a black coffee, then gestured toward Riley and Brody. "What do you guys want?"

"Oh, you're paying?" Riley grinned. He turned to the waitress, a slim woman with a nametag that read Stace. "Three bagels, a large coffee and throw in some extra butter and cream cheese. Can you pack it in to-go bags, too? Thanks."

"Two blueberry muffins and a large coffee for me," Brody said.

"You're guys aren't seriously going to eat all that, are you?" Finn fished out his wallet and paid the bill.

"Hell no. I'm getting breakfast for the next three days." Riley grinned again.

"Yeah, and considering how often you offer to pay, maybe I should have ordered a year's supply." Brody chuckled.

Finn rolled his eyes. "You two are a pain in the butt, you know that?"

"Hey, we all have our special skills," Riley said. "Except for you, because you're the oldest. You get the extra job of taking care of us."

"Last I checked you were grown adults."

"Hey, we may be grown, but some us aren't adults." Riley chuckled.

"Speak for yourself." Brody gave Riley a gentle punch in the shoulder.

Finn pocketed his change and followed his brothers over to a corner table. Since it was after nine, the breakfast crowd was beginning to peter out, leaving the diner almost empty. The smell of freshly roasted coffee and fresh baked bread filled the space.

"You know, I was just kidding," Riley said. "You don't have to take care of us. Or buy us breakfast."

"I didn't see your wallet out."

Riley grinned. "You were quicker on the draw." Then he sobered. "Seriously, sometimes you gotta take care of you."

"Yeah, you do," Brody said.

Finn looked at his brothers. "What is this? An intervention?"

Riley and Brody both grinned. "Now why would you think that?" Brody said, affecting innocence that Finn wasn't buying. His brothers clearly thought he was working too much and living too little. "This is just coffee, isn't it Riley?"

Their youngest brother nodded. A little too vigorously. "Coffee and bagels." Riley held out the bag. "Want one?"

Finn waved off the food. He glanced around the diner. Filled with booths and tables, the diner had a cozy feel. Seventies tunes played on the sound system, while Stace, apparently the lone waitress, bustled from table to table and called out orders to the short-order cook in the back. "What made you pick this place?" Finn asked. "I didn't even know you came here."

"Oh, I don't know. We thought it'd be nice to have

a change of scenery." Riley's head was down, while he fished in the bag.

"Change of scenery?" Finn tried to get Riley's attention, but his brother seemed to be avoiding him. "What is this really about?"

The bell over the door rang and Riley jerked his head up, then started smiling like a fool. He elbowed Brody. "Well, there's our cue to leave."

"What? We just got here."

Riley rose. Brody popped up right beside him, guilty grins on both McKenna faces. "Yeah, but someone much better company than us just showed up." Riley dropped the bag of food onto the table. "I'll leave these. Be nice and share."

"What? Wait!" But his brothers were already heading for the door. Finn pivoted in his seat to call after them. And stopped breathing for a second.

Ellie stood in the doorway, framed by the sun, which had touched her hair with glints of gold. She had on a dark blue dress today that skimmed her knees and flared out like a small bell. It nipped in at her waist, and dropped to a modest V in the front. She wore navy kitten heels today, but still her legs, her curves, everything about her looked amazing.

Finn swallowed. Hard.

Riley and Brody greeted Ellie, then Riley pointed across the room at Finn. Riley leaned in and whispered something to Ellie, and her face broadened into a smile. It hit Finn straight in the gut, and made his heart stop. Then Ellie crossed the room, and Finn forgot to breathe.

Her smile died on her lips when she reached him. "I didn't know you'd be here this morning."

"I didn't know, either." Finn gestured toward the door. "I suspect my brother is at work here."

"I think you're right. I've seen him in here a couple times. I recognized him from the cocktail party and we got to talking one day. I told him I'm here pretty often for my caffeine fix. I guess he figured he'd get us both in the same place."

"That's Riley." Finn shook his head. "My little brother, the eternal optimist and part-time matchmaker."

"He means well. And he thinks the world of you." She cocked her head and studied him. "Wow. You three do look a lot alike."

"Blame it on our genes." Finn wanted to leave, but at the same time, wanted to stay. But his feet didn't move, and he stayed where he was. He gestured toward the bag on the table. "Bagel? Or do you want me to get you a coffee?"

She glanced at her watch. "I have about fifteen minutes before I have to get to a meeting. I really should—" Her stomach growled, and she blushed, then pressed a hand to her gut, then glanced at the growing line at the counter. Despite the light banter, the mood between them remained tense, nearly as tough as the bagel's exterior. "Okay, maybe I have enough time for just half a bagel."

Finn opened the bag and peered inside. "Multigrain, cheese or plain?"

"Cheese, of course. If I'm going to have some carbs, I'm going all out."

"A woman after my own heart." Finn reached in the bag, pulled out a cheese-covered bagel and handed it to her, followed by a plastic knife and some butter. She laid it out on a napkin, slathered on some butter, then took a bite. When the high calorie treat hit her palate, she smiled, and Finn's heart stuttered again.

"Oh, my." Ellie's smile widened. "Delicious."

He watched her lips move, watched the joy that lit her features. "Yes. I agree."

"Oh, I'm sorry, do you want some?"

"Yes," he said. Then jerked to attention when he realized she meant the bagel. And not her. "Uh, no, I already ate this morning."

"Let me guess." She popped a finger in her mouth and sucked off a smidgen of butter. Finn bit back a groan. Damn. He wanted her. Every time he saw her, desire rushed through him.

"You had plain oatmeal," Ellie went on. "Nothing fancy, nothing sugary."

"No. Muffins."

Her brows lifted and a smile toyed with the edge of her mouth. "Not ones from the floor, I hope?"

The words brought the memory of that day in her kitchen rocketing back. Their first day as a married couple. The sexual tension sparking in the air. The desire that had pulsed in him like an extra heartbeat.

He cleared his throat. "Freshly baked and boxed," he said. "From a bakery down the street from my apartment. I rarely eat at home and usually grab something on the way to work."

"This bagel is delicious." She took another bite. Butter glistened on her upper lip, and Finn had to tell himself—twice—that it wasn't his job to lick it off.

Except she was his wife. And that was the kind of thing husbands did with wives.

Unless they were in a platonic relationship.

But were they? Really? How many times had he kissed her, touched her, desired her? Had he really thought he could have a friends-only relationship with a woman this beautiful? This intriguing? A woman who made him forget his own name half the time?

And that was the problem. If he let himself get distracted by Ellie, he'd make a foolish decision. Finn was done making those.

"Why not?" Ellie asked.

"Uh…why not what?" His attention had wandered back to the bedroom, and he forced it to the present.

"Why not eat at home?"

It was a simple question. Demanded nothing more than a simple answer, and Finn readied one, something about hating to cook and clean. But that wasn't what came out. "It's too quiet there."

Her features softened, and she lowered the bagel to the napkin. The room around them swelled with people, but in that moment, it felt like they were on an island of just two. "I know what you mean. I feel the same way about where I live. The floors echo when I walk on them. It's so…lonely."

Lonely. The exact word he would have used to describe his life, too.

A thread of connection knitted between them. Finn could feel it closing a gap, even though neither of them moved. "Have you always lived alone?"

"Pretty much. Even when I was younger, my parents were never there. My dad worked all the time and my mom…" Ellie sighed and pushed the rest of her breakfast to the side. "She had her own life. In college I did the dorm thing, but after that, I had an apartment on my own. I used to love it in my twenties, you know, no one to answer to, no one to worry about, but as I've gotten older…"

"It's not all it's cracked up to be." He wondered what had made him admit all this in a coffee shop on a bright spring day. He'd never considered himself to be a sharing kind of man. Yet with Ellie, it seemed only natural to open up. "Though it was nice to share your space for a couple of days."

Her face brightened. "Was it? Really?"

"Yeah. Really." The kind of nice he could get used to.

He ignored the warning bells ringing in his head, the alarms reminding him that the last time he'd allowed a woman to get this close, it had cost him dearly. He couldn't live the rest of his life worried that someone was going to steal his business. Riley and Brody were right. It was time for him to stop taking care of everyone else and focus on himself for a little while. Just for today.

"I agree." She toyed with the bagel. "I guess my priorities have shifted, too. I built all these houses for other people and after a while, I realized I wanted that, too."

"What?"

"You were right the other day." She lifted her gaze to his and in her eyes, he saw a craving for those intangible things other people had. "As scared as I am of falling in love, of having the kind of bad marriage my parents had, I really do want the two-point-five kids. The block parties. The fenced-in yard. Even the dog."

His coffee grew cold beside him. He didn't care. People came and went in the busy coffee shop. He didn't care. Time ticked by on his watch. He didn't care. All he cared about was the next thing Ellie Winston was going to say. "What…what kind of dog?"

"This is going to sound silly and so clichéd." She dipped her head and that blush he'd come to love filled her cheeks again.

"Let me guess. A Golden retriever?"

She gave him an embarrassed nod. "Yeah."

He shook his head and chuckled.

"What?"

"When I was a kid, I asked Santa for a dog. My mother

was allergic, so it was never going to happen, but I kept asking. Every Christmas. Every birthday. And the answer was always the same. No." He shrugged. "They got me a goldfish. But it wasn't the same."

"What kind of dog did you want?" Then her eyes met his and she smiled. "Oh, let me guess. A Golden retriever."

The thread between them tied another knot. What was it Ellie had said about a real marriage? That it was one where the two people knew each other so well, they could name their dreams and desires?

Were they turning into that?

Finn brushed the thought away. It was a coincidence, nothing more. "Billy Daniels had a Golden," he said. "It was the biggest, goofiest dog you ever saw, but it was loyal as hell to him. Every day when we got out of school, that dog would be waiting on the playground for Billy and walk home with him. Maybe because Billy always saved a little something from his lunch for a treat. He loved that dog. Heck, we all did."

"Sounds like the perfect dog."

"It seemed like it to me. Though, as my mother reminded me all the time, I wasn't the one dealing with pet hair on the sofa or dog messes in the backyard."

"True." She laughed. "So why didn't you get a dog when you grew up?"

"They're a lot of responsibility. And I work a lot. It just didn't seem fair to the dog."

"But every boy should get his dream sometime, shouldn't he?"

She'd said it so softly, her green eyes shimmering in sympathy, that he could do nothing but nod. A lump sprang in his throat. He chastised himself—they were talking about a dog, for Pete's sake. A gift he'd asked for when he was a kid. He was a grown man now, and he didn't believe in Santa anymore. Nor did he have room in his life for a dog.

What do you have room for? Riley had asked. And right now, Finn didn't know. He'd thought he had it all ordered out in neat little columns, but every time he was near Ellie, those columns got blurred.

"You know what I do sometimes?" Ellie said, leaning in so close he could catch the enticing notes of her perfume. "I go to the pet store and I just look. It gives me that dog fix for a little while."

"Maybe if I'd done that more often when I was a kid, I wouldn't have kept bothering Santa."

She got to her feet and put out her hand. "Come on, Finn. Let's go see what Santa's got in the workshop."

"What? Now? I thought you had a meeting to get to."

"It can wait a bit." To prove it, she pulled her cell phone out of her purse and sent a quick email. "There. I have an hour until they start sending out the search party."

He had a pile of work on his desk that would rival Mount Everest. Calls to return, emails to answer, bills to pay. He should get back to work and stop living in this fantasy world with Ellie. Instead he took out his phone and shot an email to his assistant. "There. I have an hour, too," he said.

"Good." She smiled. "Really good."

Finn took Ellie's hand, and decided that for sixty minutes, he could believe in the impossible.

CHAPTER TEN

ELLIE had been prepared to walk out of the diner the second she saw Finn this morning. To refuse the bagel, the offer of coffee, to just ignore him as he'd done to her for the last few days. Then Riley had leaned over and whispered, "Give him a chance. He's more of a softie than you know."

And so she'd sat down at the table, and wondered what Riley had meant. Was Finn the competitor her father had cautioned her against, or was he the man she had seen in snippets over the past days?

Today, he'd been the man she'd met in the lobby—complex and nuanced and a little bit sentimental. And she found herself liking that side of him.

Very much. Falling for it, all over again, even as her head screamed caution.

Then he'd gone and surprised her with their destination and she realized she didn't just like him a little. She liked him a lot. Finn McKenna, with his gruff exterior, was winning her over. Maybe doing a lot more than that. Even as she told herself to pull back, not to get her heart involved, she knew one thing—

Her heart was already involved with him. Ellie was falling for her husband.

The problem was, she wasn't sure he wanted to be her

husband anymore, nor was she positive she could trust him. Her father's words kept ringing in her head. *He's backed into a corner, and a dog that's in a corner will do anything to get out.*

Did Finn have a secret agenda to take over her company? Was that why he kept retreating to the impersonal? Or was he struggling like she was, with the concept of a marriage that wasn't really a marriage?

A contract, he had called it. The word still stung.

If that was all he wanted, then why was he here? What did he truly want?

"Are you two looking to add a dog to your family?"

The woman's question drew Ellie out of her thoughts. "No. Not yet. We're just looking."

Beside her, Finn concurred. He had a brochure from the animal shelter in his hand, and had deposited a generous check into the donation jar on the counter. The director of the shelter, a man named Walter, had come out to thank Finn, and engaged him in a fifteen-minute conversation about the shelter's mission. When Ellie had asked him to go to the pet store, she'd been sure he'd drive to one of the chain stores in the city. But instead he'd pulled into the parking lot of the animal shelter, and her heart had melted. Finn McKenna. A softie indeed.

Every time she told herself not to get close to him, not to take a risk on a relationship that could be over before it began, he did something like that.

"Well, we have plenty of wonderful dogs here to look at." The woman opened a steel door and waved them inside. "Take your time. I'll be right back. We're a little short-staffed today, so I need to get someone to man the phones, then I'll join you." She left the room, and as soon as the door clicked shut, the dogs took that as their cue.

A cacophony of barking erupted like a long-overdue

volcano. Down the long corridor of kennels, Ellie could see dogs of every size and breed. They pressed themselves to the kennel gates, tails wagging, tongues lolling, hope in their big brown eyes.

"Everyone wants to go home with us," Finn said as they started to walk down the row and the barking got louder. "We could be the people in *101 Dalmatians*."

We. Had that been a slip of the tongue? Or was she reading too much into a simple pronoun?

"I don't think so." Ellie laughed. "One dog would be plenty."

Finn bent down, wiggled a couple fingers into the hole of the fenced entrance and stroked a dachshund under the chin. The dog's long brown body squirmed and wriggled with joy. "Hey there, buddy."

Ellie lowered herself beside Finn and gave the little dog a scratch behind the ears. "He's a cutie."

"He is. Though…not exactly a manly dog."

"You never know. He could be a tiger at the front door."

Finn chuckled, then rose. They headed down the hall, passing a Doberman, some Chow mixes and a shaggy white dog that could have been a mix of almost every breed. Finn gave nearly every one of them a pat on the head and the dogs responded with enthusiastic instant love. Ellie's heart softened a little more. She kept trying to remind herself that she didn't want to fall for this man, didn't want to end up unhappy and lonely, trapped in a loveless marriage, but it didn't seem to work.

Finn walked on, then stopped at a cage halfway down on the right side. A middle-aged Golden retriever got to her feet and came to the door, her tail wagging, her eyes bright and interested. "Aw, poor thing," he said softly. "I bet you hate being here." The dog wagged in response. "She's a beautiful dog."

Ellie wiggled two fingers past the wire cage door and stroked the dog's ear. The Golden let out a little groan and leaned into the touch. Finn gave her snout a pat, then did the same to the other ear. The dog looked about ready to burst with happiness. Ellie reached up and retrieved the clipboard attached to the outside of the cage. "It says her name is Heidi."

"Nice name for a dog. Wonder why she's here?"

Ellie flipped the informational sheet over. It sported bright, happy decorations with lots of "Adopt Me" messages, along with a quick history of Heidi. "The paper says her owner got too old to take care of her." Ellie put the clipboard back. "That's so sad."

"Yeah. Poor thing probably doesn't understand why she's here." He gave Heidi another scratch and she pressed harder against the cage.

"Stuck in limbo, waiting for someone to bring her home." Ellie sighed. She grasped the wire bars of the cage, the metal cold and hard against her palm. The dogs in the kennel began to calm a little, their barks dropping to a dull roar, but Ellie didn't hear them. She looked into Heidi's sad brown eyes and saw another pair of sad eyes, on the other side of the world. "So tragic."

"You're not talking about the dog, are you?"

Ellie bit her lip and shook her head. "No."

Finn shifted to scratch Heidi's neck. The dog's tail went into overdrive. "Tell me about her."

Ellie glanced up at the clipboard again, scanning the information on the top sheet. "She's six years old, a female, spayed—"

"Not the dog. The little girl in China."

"You mean Jiao?" Ellie said, her heart catching in her

throat. Finn had never asked about Jiao, not once since the moment she had proposed the marriage of convenience. "You really want to know about her?"

Finn nodded. He kept on giving Heidi attention, but his gaze was entirely on Ellie. "Yeah, I do."

She wanted to smile, but held that in check. Just because Finn asked about Jiao didn't mean he wanted to be part of Jiao's life. He could be making conversation. "She's two. But really bright for her age. She loves to read books, although her version of reading is flipping the pages and making up words for what she sees." Ellie let out a laugh. "Her favorite animal is a duck, and she has this silly stuffed duck she carries with her everywhere. She's got the most incredible eyes and—" Ellie cut the sentence off. "I'm rambling. I'm sorry."

"No, please, tell me more." He got to his feet. "She's important to you and I want to know why. How did you meet her?"

Ellie searched Finn's blue eyes. She saw nothing deceitful there, only genuine interest. Hope took flight in her chest, but she held a tight leash on it. "I went to China for a conference a few years ago. But on the way to the hotel, my cabdriver took a wrong turn, and I ended up in a little village. His car overheated, and while we were waiting for it to cool down, I got out and went into this little café type place. The woman who served me was named Sun, and since I was pretty much the only customer, we got to talking. I ended up spending the entire week in that village."

"Is Sun Jiao's mother?"

Ellie nodded. Her gaze went to the window, to the bright sun that shone over the entire world. In China, it was dark right now, but in the morning, Jiao's world would be brightened by the same sun that had greeted Ellie's morning. "She was."

"Was?"

"Sun…died. Three months ago." Just saying the words brought a rush of grief to her eyes. Such a beautiful, wonderful woman, who had deserved a long and happy life. Fate, however, had other plans and now the world was without one amazing human being.

Finn put a hand on her shoulder. "Aw, Ellie, I'm so sorry. That's terrible."

She bit her lip, and forced the tears back. "That's why Jiao needs me. Over the years, I made several trips back to China and became close friends with Sun. On my last trip, Sun told me about her cancer. Because we were so close, she and I worked out an arrangement for me to adopt Jiao. And I've been trying ever since to bring Jiao home."

He turned back to the dog, and she couldn't read his face anymore. "That's really good of you."

"It's a risk. I don't know if Jiao will be happier here with me, or in China with another couple. I don't know if I'll be a good mother. I just…don't know." She wove her fingers into the fence again, and Heidi rubbed up against her knuckles.

Finn placed his hand beside hers. Not touching, but close enough that she could feel the heat from his body. "I'm sure you'll be fine. You have a certain quality about you, Ellie, that makes people feel…at home."

She met his gaze and saw only sincerity there. "Even when I drop muffins on the floor?"

"Even then." He looked at Heidi again, and gave the dog some more attention. "That's a valuable quality to have for raising a kid, you know. When your home is uncertain, it makes it hard to just be a kid."

She sensed that this was coming from someplace deep in Finn. They kept their attention on the dog, as the conversation unwound like thread from a spool. "Did you have a hard time just being a kid, Finn?"

He swallowed hard. "Yeah." He paused a moment, then went on. "I was the oldest, so I saw the most. My parents loved us, of course, but they should have never married each other. They knew each other for maybe a month before they eloped in Vegas. My mother was pregnant before they came home. My father always said he would have left if not for the kids."

"Oh, Finn, that had to be so hard on you."

"I wasn't bothered so much by that." Finn turned to Ellie, his blue eyes full of years of hard lessons. "It was that my father had fallen out of love with my mother, long, long ago, but my mother kept on holding on to this silly romantic notion that if she just tried hard enough, he'd love her again like he used to. If he ever did. So they fought, and fought, and fought, because she wanted the one thing he couldn't give her."

"His heart."

Finn nodded. "He provided money and clothes and shoes, but not the love my mother craved. I watched her cry herself to sleep so many nights. I've often wondered if…"

When he didn't go on, Ellie prodded gently. "If what?"

"If they got into an accident that night because they were fighting again." He let out a long breath. "I'll never know."

She understood so much more now about Finn. No wonder he shied away from relationships. No wonder he kept his emotions in check, and pulled himself back every time they got close. Was that why he buried himself in work? Instead of giving his heart to someone else? "You can't let that stop you from living, too."

"It doesn't."

"Are you sure about that?" she asked. He held her gaze for a moment, then broke away.

"Did you get a date for the home visit yet?"

He had changed the subject once again, pushing her away whenever she got close. Why? "Yes. I was going to call you today. Friday at eleven."

He nodded. "I'll be there."

"You will? I wasn't sure…" She bit her lip. "I didn't think you would. After what you said the other day."

"I'll be there. Because—" his fingers slipped into the thick fur on Heidi's neck again, scratching that one spot that made her groan "—no one should have to be in a place like this. No dog. No person."

She wanted to kiss him, wanted to grab him right then and there and explode with joy. But she held back, not sure where they stood on their relationship, if they even had one. Doors had been opened between them today, and Ellie was hesitant to do anything that might shut them again. "Thank you."

"You're welcome." His gaze met hers, and for a long heartbeat, it held. Then Heidi pressed against the cage, wanting more attention, and Finn returned to the dog. "You're a good girl, aren't you?"

If anyone had asked her if she had thought Finn "the Hawk" McKenna would be a dog lover who would be easily brought to his knees by a mutt in an animal shelter, she would have told them they were crazy. But in the last few days, she had seen sides of Finn she suspected few people did. And she liked what she saw. More every minute. "You really like dogs, huh?"

"Yeah." He turned to her and grinned. "Don't tell

Billy Daniels, but sometimes I snuck his dog a little of my leftover lunch, too."

She laughed and got to her feet again. "My, my, Finn. You do surprise me."

He rose and cast her a curious glance. "I do? I don't think I surprise anyone."

"You're not what I thought. Or expected."

He took a step closer, and the noise in the room seemed to drop. The dogs' barking became background sounds. "What did you expect?"

"Well, everything I heard about you said you were business only. The magazine articles, the way the other architects talked about you." What her father had said about him. Right now, she had trouble remembering any of those words. "Everything you said, too."

"My reputation precedes me," he said, his voice droll.

"But when I first met you, well, not when I *first* met you, but that day in the office, you were like that. A cool cucumber, as my grandmother would say. You didn't seem like the kind of man who would have dramatic outbursts or irrational thoughts. And from what I've seen, you're smart and good at your job."

He snorted. "That sounds boring."

"And then I see this other side of you," she went on. "This guy who makes corny jokes about Cinderella, and eats at fast food restaurants so he doesn't have to stay in an empty house, and has a soft spot in his heart for a dog he never even owned. A guy who takes a girl to an animal shelter instead of a pet store."

"I just thought, there are tons of unwanted dogs and why buy a puppy when…" He shrugged, clearly uncomfortable with the praise. "Well, it just made more sense."

"It did." She smiled, and leaned ever so slightly toward him. She wanted more of this side of Finn, more of him in general. Every moment she spent with him showed her another dimension of this man who was her husband, yet at the same time, still a stranger. A man who had been wounded by his childhood, and yet, seemed to still believe in happy endings.

The Finn she saw today—the one who pitied a dog in a shelter and realized how like Jiao's life the dog's was—that Finn was the man she was...

Well, starting to fall for. And fall hard. Damn. Every time she tried not to—

She did.

The thought caused a slight panic in her chest, but that disappeared, chased by a sweet lightness. Could she really be falling in love with her husband?

"You're a good man." Ellie smiled.

"Thank you," he said, his voice gruff, dark. He reached up a hand and cupped her jaw, and Ellie thought she might melt right then and there. God, she loved it when he touched her like that. She saw something in his eyes—something that said maybe this wasn't just a contract to him, either, despite what he'd said.

Ever so slowly, Finn closed the gap between them, winnowing it to two inches, one. His breath dusted across her lips and his sky-blue eyes held hers. Anticipation fluttered in her chest. The dogs, apparently realizing no one was interested in them right now, quieted. But Ellie's heart slammed in her chest, so fast and loud she was sure Finn could hear it.

"You are surprising, too," he said. "In a hundred ways."

"Really?"

"Really." Then he kissed her.

He took his time, his lips drifting across hers at first, tasting and tempting. Then his hand came up to cup the back of her head, tangle in her hair, and with a groan, his kiss deepened. His mouth captured hers, made it one with his, and Ellie curved into him. Finn's body pressed to hers, tight and hard, and their kiss turned breathless, hurried. Each of them tasting the other with little nips, shifting position left, right, his tongue plundering her mouth and sending a dizzying spiral of desire through her body.

This was what she had dreamed of in those nights since Finn had slipped a wedding ring on her finger. What she'd had a taste of at the courthouse, and then later on her balcony. This was what she had imagined, if the two of them had a real marriage. The heat nearly exploded inside of Ellie and she knew that if they hadn't been standing in the middle of an animal shelter, they would have been doing a lot more than just kissing.

Behind them, the dogs began barking again and Ellie drew back, the spell broken. "I can't do this."

"Why not?"

She looked into his eyes and saw the same hesitation as before. She wondered if it was true emotional fear on his part, or if her father's cautions were right. Or because she knew she was risking her heart, and he was keeping his to himself. When would she learn? "Because every time I kiss you, I only get half of you, Finn. You keep the rest of yourself locked away."

"I'm not—"

"You are. You told me yourself that you watched your parents suffer through a miserable marriage. I know that has you scared, because I saw the same thing when I was a kid, and I've done my best to avoid getting close to anyone ever since. But you know what I learned in China? What Sun taught me just before she died? That it's okay to love with your whole heart. It's okay to take that risk, even if it costs you everything. Because in the end, the people you love will be better off for having you in their hearts."

He shook his head and turned away. "Sometimes all you end up with is a broken heart."

"Just like in business, huh? Sometimes you win, and everything works out perfectly. And sometimes you lose and take a dent to the bottom line. But you can't do either if you don't take a risk."

She waited a long time for Finn to respond. But he didn't.

Because the truth hurt or because he was keeping his distance, and stringing her along just to grab the business out from under her later? The part of her that had seen Finn take pity on a shelter dog wanted to believe otherwise, but the part that had read the news reports and heard about how he nearly married another competitor's daughter, wondered.

Was she letting herself get blinded by her emotions? The very thing she'd vowed not to do?

Behind them, the door opened and the woman from the shelter stepped inside. "Did you two find anything you wanted?"

Ellie glanced back at Finn one more time. His features had returned to stoic and cold. The man she thought she'd seen earlier today was gone. If he'd ever really been there at all.

"No," she said. "There's nothing I want here. I'm sorry for wasting your time."

CHAPTER ELEVEN

FINN drove back to his office alone. By the time he reached the sidewalk—after being detoured by Walter, who stopped a second time to thank Finn for his donation—Ellie was gone. She'd either walked or taken a cab. It didn't matter. The message was clear.

She was done with him.

He should be glad. For a minute there in the shelter he had lost his head, and let his hormones dictate his decisions. He'd kissed her, allowed himself to start falling for her, and stop thinking about the smart decision. The one that would leave everyone intact at the end.

Ellie had accused him of being afraid of repeating his parent's mistakes. Hell, yes, he was afraid of that, and afraid of doing it with Jiao caught in the crossfire. The already orphaned girl had been through enough. She didn't need to watch the marriage of her new parents fall apart.

He thought of the orphaned dogs he'd seen earlier. They were all so sad, yet at the same time so hopeful. Their tails wagged, tongues lolled and their barks said they were sure these two visitors would be their new saviors.

All it required was saying yes, and opening his heart and home.

Then why had he never done that? Never adopted a dog. Never settled down, never had children. Ellie was right. He'd taken risks in everything but his personal life. And where had it gotten him?

He stepped into his office and looked at the towering stacks of work sitting in his IN box. Everything was in its place, labeled and ordered, easy to organize and dispense. This was where he felt comfortable, because here he could control the outcome.

With a marriage or with a child…there were so many opportunities to make a mess of things. Finn excelled here, in the office, and even that had turned into a disaster in the past year. What made him think he could handle a dog, or a child? Heck, except for that goldfish, he'd never even had a pet.

And even the goldfish had gone belly up within a week.

He dropped into his desk chair, and let out a sigh. He dove into the piles of papers stacked beside him and spent a solid two hours whittling it down from a mountain to a molehill but work didn't offer the usual solace. If anything, the need to be in the office grated on him, and made him feel like he was missing out on something important.

"Hey, Finn, how's married life?"

Finn looked up and grinned at Charlie, then waved his friend into his office. "What are you doing here?"

"Had some business to take care of in Boston." He thumbed toward the street. "Remember my aunt Julia, who lived here?" Finn nodded. "Well, she died last month, and her will's just been a mess over at probate."

"I'm sorry to hear that."

"It's no big deal. It gives me a chance to come back and see some of the guys from the old neighborhood."

Charlie settled into one of the visitor's chairs and propped his ankle on his knee. "I miss having you guys around. The four of us got into a lot of trouble."

Finn chuckled. The McKenna boys and Charlie had been the neighborhood wild children, whooping it up until their mothers called them in for supper. "We did indeed."

"Then we all grew up and got serious. Well, all of us except for Riley."

"I don't think Riley's ever going to grow up. He's the perpetual kid."

"Sometimes that's good for us." Charlie gestured toward Finn. "Besides, who are you to talk? You *eloped*, my man. If I didn't marry you myself, I never would have believed it."

Finn waved it off. "Temporary moment of insanity."

"I met your wife, remember? I gotta say, I think that was the smartest decision you ever made in your life."

"Smartest, huh?" It hadn't felt so smart lately. He had married a woman, thinking he could keep it all about business. Considering how many times he'd kissed her, he'd done a bad job of business only. It was as if he was drawn to the very thing that scared him the most—an unpredictable, heady relationship fueled by passion, not common-sense conclusions.

"She's perfect for you, Finn. Intelligent, beautiful, funny. And willing to marry *you*."

"Hey. I'm not that bad."

"No, not *that* bad." Charlie grinned. "But, I've known you all your life and you can be a bit…difficult."

"Difficult?"

"Yeah, as in a mule in the mud. In business, that's served you well. You put your head down, plow through any obstacles and don't take no for an answer. And look where you are today." Charlie waved at Finn's office. "Up on top of the world, overlooking the city of Boston. Doesn't get much better than that."

"I don't know. I had a bad year last year."

Charlie waved it off. "Lucy did her damage, yes, but in the end, it toughened you up, made you a better businessman. If you never had any failures to knock you down, you'd never be able to appreciate the successes that bring you back up."

Finn took in the city below him, then thought of the company he had built from the ground up. Sure, he'd suffered a pretty bad setback last year, but overall, he was still in business and still doing what he loved. "True."

"And really, you didn't fail. You just met someone who is exactly like you." Charlie chuckled. "A Hawkette."

Finn thought about that for a second. Was that where all his careful planning, detailed lists and sensible dating got him? He'd tried so hard to find someone who was similar to him in personality, career and goals, and it had backfired. He'd tried to mitigate the risk by being smart—

And in the process, made an even bigger mistake. "I did, didn't I?"

"Yep. That's why I think this Ellie is good for you. She's sunshine to your storm clouds."

"I'm not that bad. Am I?"

"Nah. But you could use someone who rounds you out, Finn. You've always been a practical guy and when you're running a business based on straight lines, that's important. But when it comes to the heart, man—" Charlie thumped his own chest for emphasis "—you gotta follow the curves."

"Maybe you're right."

"Hey, I'm a judge. I'm always right." Charlie grinned.

"So, how are the kids?" Finn asked, just to change the subject.

"Perfect, as always." Charlie beamed. "But then again, I'm a little biased."

Finn could see the joy and pride in Charlie's face. He'd known Charlie since elementary school, and had never seen his friend this happy. He seemed to have it all—a great career, a wonderful wife, incredible kids. He and Finn had started in the same place, grown up side by side, followed similar paths—college, then starting at the bottom and working their way up—that it made Finn wonder if maybe there was some secret to having it all that he was missing. "Don't you worry about messing it up?"

"Of course I do. Being a husband and a father is the biggest risk of all because you have other people's lives in your hands. But in the end, it's so worth it." Charlie had pulled out his wallet and was flipping proudly through the pictures of his kids. "This is what it's all about, my friend. Sophie just lost her two front teeth, and she goes around whistling everywhere. Max signed up for T-ball…"

Finn wasn't listening. He was looking at the clear love in Charlie's face, the determination to do right by his kids, and realized where he had seen that look before.

On Ellie's face. When she talked about Jiao.

She was scared to take the risk of being Jiao's parent, but she was doing it anyway. Clearly Ellie loved this little girl. Finn had no doubt she'd be a good mother. For a second, he envied her that love, that clear conviction that she could raise a child she barely knew. He was sure she would be a terrific mother. Any child would be blessed to be raised by a woman as amazing as Ellie Winston.

As Finn watched one of his oldest and best friends

talk about the wondrous joy a family could bring to a man's life, he felt a stab of envy. Ellie was his temporary wife, and after all this was over, there would be no pictures or bragging or stories to tell.

He glanced at the clock and realized there was one thing he could do before they got divorced. He could help her bring that child home.

And make sure Ellie's floors would no longer echo.

CHAPTER TWELVE

ELLIE had spent the better part of Friday morning scrubbing her house from top to bottom. Cleaning helped distract her, helped take her mind off the worries about work, the home visit today, and the worries about Jiao. She had called the orphanage earlier and been assured that Jiao was fine and healthy, but that didn't help set Ellie's mind at ease when it came to her daughter's future. Every hour that ticked by with Jiao stuck in adoption limbo was undoubtedly hurting her emotionally.

When she wasn't worrying about the adoption, her mind was on Finn. For a while there, she'd thought they were building something. She'd thought...

Well, it didn't matter what she'd thought. Finn had made it clear over and over again that he wasn't interested in a relationship with her. There was the home visit today, and then the hospital plans were due to be delivered to the client on Tuesday, and after that, she was sure their alliance would end. Probably a good thing, she told herself.

Tears rushed to her eyes but she willed them back. Finn was the one losing out, not her. She told herself that a hundred times as she scoured the shower walls. But the tears still lingered.

A little after ten-thirty that morning, her doorbell

rang. Ellie peeled off her rubber gloves, dropped them into a nearby bucket, then ran downstairs to answer it. Finn stood on the other side.

"You came."

"I promised you I would." He was wearing a light blue golf shirt and a pair of jeans that outlined his lean, defined legs. The pale color of his shirt offset his eyes, and made them seem even bluer. Her body reacted the same as always to seeing him—a nervous, heated rush pumping in her veins—even as her head yelled caution.

"Thank you."

"No need to thank me." He gave her a grin, that lop-sided smile that made her heart flip. "I'm here to help you get ready. Not that I'm a whole lot of help in the home department, but I figured you'd be a wreck, and need a hand getting things done."

He could have been reading her mind. Joy bubbled inside her, but she held it back, still cautious and reserved. This was everything she'd ever wanted. Finn would be a temporary husband, just as she'd planned, he'd do the home visit with her, then go back to living his own life, leaving her and Jiao alone, to form their own little family of two. She should have been happy.

Then why did she feel so…empty? *Focus on Jiao. On bringing her home. Not on what will never be with Finn.*

"That sounds good," she said. "Thank you."

"We don't have much time before they arrive," Finn said. "And a lot to do. So let's get to work." Finn grabbed a box that she hadn't noticed beside his feet. "I brought a few more of my things to put around the house, so it looks more like I'm living here. I didn't bring enough before."

"Good idea."

"I was just trying to think through all possible angles.

People will expect us to have commingled belongings. I brought some clothing, the two photographs I have of myself, and a six-pack of beer."

She laughed at the beer. "That sounds like a typical male."

"That was my intent. I want to make sure we have maximum plausibility."

Disappointment drowned out her hope. This whole thing wasn't about Finn being thoughtful, it was about him being methodical and thorough, covering all his bases. Just when she thought the Hawk had disappeared...he came to the forefront again. She wondered again if this was true help, or a calculated move to help his business.

She'd focus on the adoption, and worry about the rest later. Linda would be here soon and Ellie only had this one shot to convince her and the social worker that Jiao would be happy here.

"You should probably put your things in my bedroom," she said.

"Yeah." His gaze met hers in one long, heated moment. She turned away first, sure that if she looked at him for one more second, she'd forget all the reasons she had for not getting involved with him.

"Why don't I help you?" She turned on her heel and led Finn up the stairs, trying not to think about how surreal this all was. She was taking her husband to her bedroom, for the sole purpose of pretending she shared the room with him. In the end, he'd pack up his things and be out of her life. Forever.

"I already moved the things you left behind in the guest room into here," she said. "I didn't know if you'd be here today and I guess I wanted to set up maximum plausibility, too."

"We think alike." He grinned. "Maybe that's a good thing."

"Maybe." She opened the door to the master bedroom, then followed Finn inside. Then she turned back and laid a light hand on his arm. "If I don't get a chance to tell you later, thank you."

He shrugged, like it was no big deal. "You're welcome."

"No, I mean it, Finn. This is huge for me, and I really, really appreciate you helping with this."

His eyes meet hers, and she felt the familiar flutter in her chest whenever he looked at her. "You're very welcome, Ellie."

The moment extended between them. Her heart skipped a beat. Another.

Behind her, Ellie was painfully aware of the bed. The wedding rings on their hands. If this had been any other marriage, they would be in that bed together, every night, making love. If this had been any other marriage, she would have stepped into Finn's arms, lifted her face to his and welcomed another of his earth-shattering kisses.

If this had been any other marriage...

But it wasn't. And she needed to stop acting like it was.

She spun around and crossed to the closet. "Uh, let me shift some of my clothes over, and we can fit yours in there." She opened one of the double doors and pushed several dresses aside, the hangers rattling in protest, then she turned back to Finn. He was smiling. "What?"

"Hootie & the Blowfish." He pointed at her closet.

She turned back and saw the concert T-shirt hanging in her closet. It had faded over the years, but still featured the band's name in big letters on the front. "Oh my. I forgot that was in there. That was oh, almost fifteen years ago." She pulled out the hanger and fingered the soft cotton shirt. "I don't know why I hung on to it for so long."

"Did you hear them in concert?"

"Yep. Me and two of friends went. We were both hoping to marry Darius Rucker. They were my favorite band, and I figured I could hear Hootie songs every day if I married the lead singer."

He chuckled. "I guess that didn't work out."

"Kinda hard to catch his eye when we're in the fortieth row." She laughed, then clutched the shirt to her chest. "Do you like Hootie & the Blowfish?"

He nodded. "I went to a concert, too, one of their last ones before Rucker branched out on his own."

She propped a fist on her hip. "Yes, but do you have the T-shirt to prove it?"

He dug in the box and pulled out a threadbare brown T. Laughter exploded from Ellie when she read the familiar name on the front.

"I saw them at the Boston Garden," he said.

"Providence for me." She flipped over her shirt to show the concert information. "We could go out as twins."

"Uh, yeah...no." He laughed. "I think that would be more damaging than anything. People would think we're crazy."

"Oh, it might be fun. And get people talking."

She remembered the first time she'd said that. It had been back in the office, on their first day as a married couple. They'd shared lunch in the outdoor courtyard, and for a little while, it had felt so real, as if they were any other couple sneaking in an afternoon date. And the time they had spent in her house, had seemed real, too. Had they been pretending? Or had a part of it been a true marriage? And why did she keep hoping for the very thing she told herself she didn't want?

Finn moved closer to her, and the distance between them went from a foot to mere inches. Ellie's heart began to race. Damn, this man was handsome.

"They already are talking," he said.

"Really? And what do you think they're saying?"

His gaze locked on hers. Ellie's pulse thundered in her head and anticipation sent a fierce rush through her veins. She held her breath, waiting on his words, his touch.

A slight smile curved across his lips. "I think they're saying that they can't believe I married you."

"Because I'm such a bad match for you?"

"No. Because you are such an amazing woman." He reached up and drifted his fingers along her jawline, sliding across her lips. She nearly melted under that touch, because it was so tender, so sensual. "Smart and funny and sexy and a hundred other adjectives."

"Finn…" She drew in a breath, fought for clarity. Every time she thought she understood Finn and his motives, he threw a curveball at her. Was he here for business, or something more? Was there anything between them besides an architectural alliance? A *contract*? Because right now, it sure as hell felt like something more. A lot more. And oh, how she wanted that more. She was tired of being afraid of falling in love, afraid of risking her heart. She did want the whole Cinderella fantasy, damn it, and she wanted it with Finn. The trouble was, she didn't know what he wanted.

"Every time I see you, I stop thinking—" he leaned in closer, and her heart began to race "—about anything but how much I want to kiss you again."

"Really?" The hope blossomed again inside her. Lord, she was in deep.

His fingers did a slow dance down her neck. Her nerves tingled, chasing shivers along her veins. "Really." Then finally, when she thought she could stand the wait no longer, he kissed her.

This kiss started out slow, easy, sexy, like waltzing across the floor. Then the tempo increased, and the spark between them became an inferno, pushing Ellie into Finn, searching, craving, more of him. She curved her body into his and the inferno roared down every part of them that connected. His hands roamed her back, sliding along the soft cotton of her T-shirt, then slipped over the denim of her jeans, sending a rush of fire along her back, her butt. Oh, God, she wanted him. She arched into him, opening her mouth wider, her tongue tangoing with his. Insistent, pounding desire roared through her veins. *More, more, more,* she thought. *More of everything.*

"Oh, God, Ellie," he said, his voice a harsh, low groan. Then, one, or maybe both of them began to move and in tandem, they stepped back, two steps, three, four, until Ellie's knees bumped up against the bed and they fell onto it in a tangle of arms and legs.

Finn covered her legs with one of his, never breaking the kiss. His mouth had gone from easy waltz to hot salsa, and Ellie thought she might spontaneously combust right then and there if she didn't have more of Finn. Of his kiss, his touch, his body. Damn, his body was hard in all the right places, and on top of hers, and sending her mind down the path of making love. His hand slid under her T-shirt, igniting her bare skin. She moaned, rose up to his touch, then gasped when his fingers brushed against her nipple. She gasped, arched again, and his fingers did it again. Oh, God. Even through the lacy fabric of her bra, she could feel every touch, every movement.

She murmured his name, then wrapped a leg around his hips, pressing her pelvis to his hard length. God, it had been so long since she had been with a man, so long since she had been kissed. She wanted Finn's clothes off. Wanted his naked body against hers. Wanted him inside her.

Finn seemed to know everything about her. Every touch stoked the fire inside her, every kiss added to the desire coursing through her veins, clouding her every thought. Then as she shifted to allow him more access, the clock downstairs began to chime the hour.

Ellie jerked back to the present. What was she doing? Where was she going to go with this? Was she letting her hormones overrule her brain again? She shifted away from him and scrambled to her feet. "Why are you doing this?" she asked.

"Because I want you. Because you're the most beautiful woman I've ever met. Because—"

"No. Why are you helping me? Why are you here today for the home visit?" The clock downstairs chimed ten, then eleven times, and fell silent.

"Because I made you a promise." His sky-blue eyes met hers and when he spoke his voice was quiet, tender. "And because when you were telling me about Jiao at the animal shelter, I saw how much you loved her. Every child should have a parent who loves them like that. Who would move heaven and earth to provide them with a safe and loving environment."

"Is that all there is? No hidden agenda to steal WW out from under me?"

He looked surprised. No, he looked hurt, and she wanted to take the words back. "You think that's why I did all this? Really? After everything?"

"You told me yourself that your company has had a bad year and that you were desperate to recoup the business you had lost. Desperate enough to marry the daughter of your competitor?" She bit her lip, and pushed the rest out. She didn't want him here if in the end he was going to take away the very thing her father treasured. Nothing was worth that price. "Like you almost did before?"

"Is that what you think? That I go around town marrying the competition to try to build my business up? That the Hawk swoops in and drops engagement rings to lure them in?"

She crossed her arms over her chest. "I don't know, Finn. You tell me."

"I don't. The fact that you and Lucy both work in the industry is a coincidence."

"Is it? Because it seems to me that marrying me has given your business an advantage and I want to be sure my father's company is protected."

He cursed. "Ellie, I didn't marry you for your father's company. And I have no intentions of stealing it."

"Is that what you told Lucy, too?"

The doorbell began to ring. Linda was here. Ellie cursed the timing. "We'll have to finish this later."

"Okay." He turned to the box and quickly stowed the rest of his clothes in her closet. Finn finished hanging up his clothes, then turned to the dresser and nightstand to put out a few of his personal items. Ellie crossed to the door of the bedroom and took one last look at the closet that held the incongruity of her life. Finn McKenna's dress shirts and pants hung beside her dresses, making it look like her husband was truly a part of her life.

When that was as far from the truth as could be.

Two hours later, Linda and the social worker finished their visit at Ellie's house. As they were heading out the door, Linda leaned her head back in and shot Ellie a smile. "This went great. Thanks to both of you for being available on such short notice."

"You're welcome. It was our pleasure," Finn said. He shook hands again with Linda, then took his place beside Ellie, slipping an arm around her waist. Still playing the happy couple, and after a couple hours of it, it was beginning to feel natural. Hell, it had felt natural from the minute he'd said "I do."

"We'll get the report off to the orphanage in China and from there it should only be a few days." Linda beamed. "I'm so excited for the two of you. I'm sure Jiao will be very, very happy in her new home."

Ellie thanked Linda again, then said goodbye. After the two women were gone, she closed the door and leaned against it. Finn stepped back, putting distance between them again. The charade, after all, was over. He should have been relieved.

He wasn't.

He realized that this was it. They had finished the preliminary drawings for the hospital project and save for one more meeting to go over a few details, the business side of their alliance was done. And now, with the social worker gone and the home visit over, the personal side of their partnership was over, too. He had no other reason to see Ellie again.

And that disappointed him more than he had expected.

"Thank you again," Ellie said. "You were fabulous. Really believable."

"You're welcome."

"I loved how you managed to slip in that thing about us sharing the same favorite band, and the stories about how we both saw them in concert. I think it's the details that really make a difference."

"Yeah, they do." That damned disappointment kept returning. Was it just because they'd shared an amazingly hot kiss—and a little more—back in the bedroom? Or was it because they'd been pretending so well, it had begun to feel real, and now he was mourning the loss of a relationship that had never really existed? One that he had been doing his best to avoid? "I, uh, should get going."

Her smile slipped a little. "Okay. I'll, uh, see you Monday. At the meeting."

"Sure, sounds good." He picked his keys up from the dish by the front door—another realistic touch that he had added—and pressed the remote start for his car.

"Do you want to take your stuff now?"

"Maybe I should leave it. In case they come back."

"Oh, yeah, sure. Good idea." She paused. "Are you sure there isn't anything you need?"

"No, I'm good. Oh, wait. I left my wallet on the nightstand." He thumbed toward the stairs. "Is it okay if I go up and get it?"

"Sure. This is your house, too. At least for show."

He chuckled, but the sound was empty, the laughter feigned. This wasn't his house and even though he'd pretended to for a little while, he wasn't living here anymore. He headed up the stairs and into her room.

He paused inside the doorway and took in the room one last time. A fluffy white comforter dominated her king-sized bed. Thick, comfortable pillows marched down the center of the bed, ending with a round decorative pillow in a chocolate-brown. Sheer white curtains hung at her windows, dancing a little in the slight breeze. In one corner a threadbare tan armchair sat beside a table with a lamp. Close to a dozen books stood in a towering stack on the table. Finn crossed to them, smiling at the architectural design books, then noting the mysteries and thrillers that filled out the pile. Two of them were on his own nightstand.

They listened to the same music. Read the same books. Worked in the same field. Everything pointed to them being perfect for each other.

Except…

His gaze skipped to the bed. There was a fire between them, one he couldn't ignore. It made him crazy, turned his thoughts inside out and made him do things he had never done before—like elope.

Risk.

That's what marrying Ellie had been. A huge risk. And Finn, the man who never made a move that wasn't well thought out and planned, had taken that risk with both eyes wide-open. He glanced at a picture of Ellie posing with a smiling, gap-toothed two-year-old girl with dark almond eyes and short black hair. Jiao. The two of them looked happy together, already resembling the family they would soon become.

A part of him craved to be in that circle, with Ellie and Jiao. Wanted to form a little family of three. That was the biggest risk of all, wasn't it?

He'd taken it in the last few days and realized that every time he was with Ellie, he felt a happiness he'd never known before. A lightness that buoyed his days. Was he…falling for her?

And was he doing it too late?

Finn grabbed his wallet and turned to leave. Ellie stood in the doorway, watching him. "You never answered my question."

He sighed and dropped onto the bed. Did she really think the worst of him? That he was the Hawk, through and through? "I didn't propose to Lucy with the intention of stealing her company. I proposed to her because I thought she was the right one to settle down with."

Ellie hung back by the door. "The love of your life?"

He snorted. "Far from it. She was the one who met all the mental pros and cons I had listed in my head for a relationship. She fit my little checklist, so I told myself we'd be happy. And you know what?" He shook his head, and finally admitted the truth to himself. "I was never happy with her. I was content."

"Is that so bad?"

"It's horrible. Because you never have that rush of joy hit your heart when you see the person you love." His gaze met hers, and a whoosh ran through him. "You never hurry home because you can't wait to see her smile. You never catch yourself doodling her name instead of writing a contract. You never feel regret for leaving her instead of staying to the very end." He rose and crossed to Ellie. "The most impetuous thing I did was propose to Lucy—I rushed out and bought the ring at the end of the day. After I'd compiled a list of pros and cons." He shook his head and let out a breath. "Who does that? Pros and cons?"

"Some people. I guess."

"She didn't expect me to show up at her office, and definitely didn't expect me to propose. When I got there, I walked in on a meeting with her and my biggest client. In that instant, I knew that the whole thing had been a fraud. My gut had been warning me, but I'd been too busy being practical and sensible to listen."

"What was your gut saying?"

"That she didn't love me and I didn't love her, and that I was making the biggest mistake of my life. After I broke it off, she smeared my name all over town. Made it her personal mission to steal the rest of my clients." He looked deep into her green eyes. "You were right. I am afraid of risking my heart. But then again, so are you."

"Me? I'm not afraid." But her eyes were wide and her breath was quickened. He had hit a nerve, clearly.

"Really? Then why did you do your best to push me away?"

"This isn't going anywhere. You said so yourself."

He reached up as if he was going to touch her cheek, but his hand fell away. "And you accused me of being here to steal the company."

"Are you?"

"You know that answer already. Quit trying to put up walls that don't exist."

"I didn't…" She bit her lip.

"You did and so did I. It was all so easy, because we both kept saying this marriage had an end date. You did the same thing as me, Ellie. You got close, you backed away. Got close, backed away. I think you're just as scared as I am."

"I'm not."

"Really?" He leaned in closer. "Then what would you say if I said let's not end this?"

"Didn't…end the marriage? But that was the deal."

"I realized something today when I was here, in your house, pretending to be your husband for the last time." He caressed her cheek with his thumb. "The whole time

I was wishing it was real. Because the time I've spent with you has been the best damned time of my life."

Fear shimmered in her eyes. Fear of being hurt, of letting go. Of trusting. When it came right down to it, Ellie was just as scared as he was of opening her heart. "Oh, Finn. I don't know what you want me to say."

"That you're ready to take that risk, too. That you want more than just the fiction."

She just shook her head. Finn released Ellie, then walked out the door, finally leaving behind a fairy tale that wasn't going to end with happily ever after.

CHAPTER THIRTEEN

ELLIE's heart sang with the words the doctor had just said. *Great recovery. Going home soon. Should be okay to resume limited activities.* Her father had surpassed medical expectations and was going to be all right. He'd be on a limited schedule, of course, but he would be alive, and that was all Ellie cared about.

"You're doing fabulous, Dad," Ellie said. "The doctor is thrilled with your recovery." Henry was sitting up today, looking much heartier than last time. The color had returned to his face, and he appeared to have put back on some of the weight he had lost while he was sick. In the next bed, his new roommate was watching a reality show about wild animals.

"I'm just trying to do what I'm told," Henry said.

She laughed. "For the first time in your life?"

He chuckled. "Yeah." He patted the space beside him on the bed. "Come. Sit down and tell me how things are going for you."

"Good. Well, great." Except for the fact that she hadn't talked to Finn since that day at her house, things were great. She should have been relieved that the marriage was over, but she wasn't. A part of her wondered if maybe Finn was right—if she had let him walk away because it was easier than taking the risk of asking him to stay. "The McKenna team worked with us to draw up the plans for the Piedmont hospital project. We submitted them to the client on time, and the initial review was really positive. But that's not the really good news…"

"What?"

"Well, you're about to be a grandfather." She smiled. "Jiao will be here in a few days."

A smile burst across his face. "Honey, that's wonderful! And while I'm excited to hear such good news about the business, I'm more excited about your addition to the family." He reached for the sheet of doctor's recommendations sitting on his end table and showed them to his daughter. "You can bet I'll be sticking to every one of these rules because I want to take my new granddaughter to the zoo and the park and wherever else she wants to go."

Ellie sat back, surprised at this change in her father, a man who'd never had time for those things before, a man who had stubbornly lived by his own rules—which was part of what had made him so unhealthy. "Wow. Really?"

"Really." His face softened, and he took her hand. "I missed all that with you, because all I ever did was work. Lying here in this bed has given me a lot of time to think, to regret—"

"Dad, I grew up just fine. You don't need to have regrets."

"I do. And I will. I want you to know how sorry I am that I missed out on your soccer games and band performances and prom nights." His face crumpled and tears glistened in his eyes. "Aw, Ellie, I should have been there more, and I…I wasn't."

She gave his fingers a squeeze and sent God a silent prayer of gratitude for this second chance with her father. "It's okay. We're building a great relationship now, and that's all that matters."

"No, it isn't." He let out a long sigh. "Once I'm out of this hospital, I have a lot to make up for with you, starting with asking you to move up here and take over the business. I never should have done that."

"Dad, I love architecture. I love this industry."

"But you don't love commercial buildings. I knew that, and still I asked you to take over my business." His green eyes met hers. So like her own, and filled with decades more of wisdom and experience. "You were happy designing houses."

She was, but she wasn't about to tell her dad that. She would never complain about stepping in for him at WW. It was a family business, and when your family needed you, you went. Simple as that. "You're my father. You were sick. You needed me. I didn't mind."

"I know you didn't, and that's the problem. You are too good of a daughter, Ellie girl." He sighed. "That's why I want you to quit."

"Quit? What? Dad, you're in no condition to run the company yourself. Not now." She didn't add the words *maybe never*. Because there was hope, and she wanted her father to hold on to that. "I'll stay until you come back and—"

"No." His voice was firm, filled with the strident tones people usually associated with Henry Winston. His heart might be weak but his personality and resolve remained as strong as ever. "You have a daughter to raise. You go do that."

She laughed. "Dad, I still need to pay my bills. I'll keep working and we'll work it out."

"No. I want you to quit WW Architectural Design… and start your own division. A residential division. Bring those beautiful houses you designed in the South to the Boston area. And hire lots of great people to work under you so that you don't have to put in the kind of hours I did."

"A residential division?" A thrill ran through her at the thought of getting back to designing houses again, to return to the work that had given her so much reward. "But who will run the commercial side?"

"Larry and...Finn McKenna."

Had she heard him wrong? When had Finn come into the mix? "Finn McKenna? Why? I thought you didn't trust him."

"You told me he was smart, and capable. So I gave him a call this morning," Henry said. "He told me all about how you two collaborated on the hospital project and how well it went for everyone. I never really got to know Finn before, only knew him by reputation, but now I realize I was wrong about him. He may be a tough businessman, but he's also a nice guy. Cares a lot about you."

She let out a gust at that. "He cares about his business."

"He cares about a lot more than that, but I'll let you find that out for yourself."

Was the Finn she had started to fall for the real man? Or was he the Hawk that had pushed her away a hundred times? She couldn't think about that now, she decided, not with her father to worry about, and Jiao arriving any day.

Her father shifted in the bed, and Ellie realized Henry looked a hundred times better now than he had when he'd first been admitted. It was as if having this taste of something to do had given him a new energy and it showed in his face.

"Are you sure about wanting me to quit?" she asked.

Working in residential design again, particularly if she didn't have to be there full-time, would give her the flexibility she needed to raise Jiao. She'd be able to have time with her daughter, something the little girl was going to need after such a traumatic year. It was a gift beyond measure, and she couldn't begin to thank her father enough.

He reached out and drew his daughter into a warm hug. "I don't want to see you make the same mistakes I did. I want you to watch your daughter grow up. And I want to have the time to watch her grow up, too. I didn't build this business just to watch you repeat my mistakes."

Ellie tightened her grip on her father. Tears slid down her cheeks, moistened the sleeve of his hospital gown. "You didn't make any mistakes, Dad. Not a single one."

Finn had stayed away for weeks. He'd told himself it was easier this way, that he could wean himself off Ellie Winston, and forget all about her. If that was the case, then why had he gone to see her father? Agreed to the idea of joining their companies? And heading up the new venture?

Because he was crazy. Doing that would put him in the same building as Ellie every day, and he'd known that going into this deal. He just hadn't been able to let go, even as every day he looked at his To Do list and saw "call lawyer" at the top. Procrastination had become his middle name.

Either way, it didn't matter. By the time he had the particulars in place and had set up a space in the more spacious offices of WW Architectural Design, Ellie was gone. On maternal leave, he'd been told. Her assistant went on for a good ten minutes about Ellie's trip to

China, and her new daughter. Every day he heard another tidbit about Ellie and Jiao.

And every day it felt like someone had cut out his heart and put it on a shelf.

Now he stood at the entrance to a small playground carved out of the limited green space near Ellie's neighborhood. Bright red, yellow and blue playground equipment dominated the center of the space, flanked by matching picnic tables and chairs. Green trees stood like sentries inside the wrought-iron fence. The musical sound of children laughing and playing carried on the air.

Finn's gaze skipped over the mothers sitting in clusters, chatting while their children played. Past the kids playing tag in the courtyard. Past the tennis players working up a sweat on the court next door. Then he stopped, his breath caught in his throat, when he saw her.

Ellie, sitting on a blanket, with Jiao beside her, and Jiao's stuffed duck flopped against the young girl's leg. They were having a picnic lunch, the little dark-haired girl giggling as Ellie danced animal crackers against her palm. The two of them formed a perfect circle of just them. Beside her, Linda stood and watched, a happy smile on her face. The two women chatted for a moment longer and then Linda left.

As she headed for the exit, she saw Finn and stepped over to him. "Why hello, Finn."

He gave the dark-haired woman a smile. "Hi, Linda. Nice to see you again."

"How have you been?"

"Good." Finn's gaze kept darting toward Ellie and Jiao. He'd missed Ellie's smile. A hell of a lot.

Linda thumbed toward Ellie. "You know, you really should go over there and meet Jiao. She's a wonderful little girl."

Finn opened his mouth, shut it again. He wasn't sure what to say. If he admitted he'd never seen Jiao before, then Linda would know the marriage had been a farce and maybe that would cost Ellie. Maybe even undo the adoption Ellie had worked so hard to bring to fruition.

Linda put a hand on Finn's arm. "Don't worry. I already figured it out."

"You did? How? Was it because I didn't go to China with Ellie?"

Linda laughed. "No, it was something much more simple. Your shoes."

"My shoes?"

"When we came by the house, you had clothes in the closet and a wallet on the bedside table, but not a single pair of shoes anywhere. I had had my suspicions about Ellie's fast marriage, but I didn't say anything."

Damn. He couldn't believe he'd missed such a simple detail. He'd thought he'd covered everything. He'd almost ruined the most important thing in Ellie's life. "Why? I thought Ellie had to be married to adopt Jiao."

"She did. And she was. I told the Chinese orphanage that her husband had to stay in America for a family emergency, so they didn't wonder why you didn't come to China to pick up Jiao. Either way, I knew that with or without a spouse on paper, Ellie was going to be a fabulous mother." Linda glanced over her shoulder at Ellie and her daughter. "She loves that little girl more than life itself. That's a blessing."

"I agree." The two of them seemed to go together like peas and carrots. Envy stirred in Finn's gut. He had never felt more on the outside than he did right now. Ellie had everything she'd ever wanted, and it hurt to realize that didn't include him. Perhaps if he had handled things differently, they wouldn't be here right now.

Maybe he shouldn't have married her at all. If they'd kept things entirely on a business level, then he wouldn't have this deepening ache in his chest for a life he never really lived. This stabbing regret for a relationship that had slipped away.

"You know, it's a scary thing," Linda said.

"What is?"

"Giving your heart away. Ellie did that, not knowing if she was going to be able to bring Jiao home. But she took that risk, and put everything on the line, because she loved that little girl." Linda's gaze met his. "And I think you took a big risk, too."

"Me?" He snorted. "I didn't do anything."

"You married her and stood up as her husband when she needed you most. That's a risk. And you gotta ask yourself why you did it."

"Because she needed me." He watched Ellie with Jiao, their faces close together as they laughed over something. It was the perfect picture of maternal love. Yes, he'd done the right thing in helping Ellie. In that, he took comfort.

"Maybe," Linda said. "And maybe you did it for more than just that. Maybe if she believes that, she'll take that risk, too." Then she patted him on the shoulder. "I've got to get back to work. Enjoy your family."

Linda was gone before Finn could tell her that this wasn't his family. Not at all. And no amount of wishing would make it so.

He was about to turn away when a dozen kids from a daycare center came bursting into the playground, and Finn stepped aside to let them through. Ellie looked up at the sudden noise of the newcomers. Her eyes widened when she saw him. She'd seen him, and leaving was out of the question.

He crossed the park to Ellie. "Hi."

There couldn't possibly be a lamer opening than that. All these weeks, he'd thought of what he'd say when he saw her again. "Hi" wasn't on the list at all.

She looked up at him, sunglasses covering those green eyes he loved so much. "What are you doing here?"

"I'm…" He hadn't played that out in his head, either. "Looking for you."

Better to start with the truth than to make up something. Besides, his lying skills were pretty awful. And where had lying gotten him so far anyway? Still stuck in his empty apartment, staring at the wedding band sitting on his nightstand, wondering if he'd made a huge mistake by letting her go.

Beside Ellie, Jiao bounced up and down, saying something that sounded sort of like "cracker." Ellie smiled, then placed another animal cracker in Jiao's palm, keeping an eye on her daughter while the toddler ate the treat. "How did you know where I'd be?"

"The women at the office are always talking about you and your daughter. They fell in love with her, I think."

Ellie grinned and chucked Jiao gently under the chin. "That's easy to do."

"Anyway, they said you come here almost every day."

"Jiao loves to be outside. I think it's because she was inside for so many months at the orphanage. So we try to make it here every morning." Ellie gave her daughter a tender glance, then turned back to Finn. "Why were you looking for me? Is there something going on at the office we need to talk about? Because really, Larry is your go-to guy on the commercial side, now that I'm handling residential."

It stung that she thought the only reason he would seek her out was because of work. But then again, when

had he ever made it about the personal? He'd always re-
treated behind the facade of the job. "I wanted to see
how you were doing."

"We're fine. I should be back at work next week, but
just part-time. Heading up the new division."

He'd heard all about Ellie's move into the housing sec-
tor from her father. He'd spent a lot of time talking to
Henry Winston in the last few weeks, and found he liked
Ellie's father a lot. He was becoming not just a friend to
Finn, but also a sort of surrogate father. "I know."

"How are things going with the merger?"

"Pretty smooth. Your father had a phone conference
meeting with all the employees to explain the changes.
I think that helped set some minds at ease." They were
still talking about business, and Finn knew he should
reroute the conversation, but as always, he stayed in his
comfort zone.

"How's the Piedmont project going?" Jiao, content
with her cookie, climbed into Ellie's lap and laid her head
on Ellie's shoulder. Ellie rubbed a circle of comfort onto
Jiao's back. Finn watched, seeing the obvious love Ellie
had for her new daughter. Jiao was clearly comfortable
with Ellie, too, and snuggled against her adoptive mother
as if they'd always been a family.

He started relating the details of the hospital project, all the while thinking that this was what they had
become. Colleagues who worked at the same company.
There was no hint of the woman he had been married
to in her voice, no flirtation in her smile. It was just two
co-workers having an ordinary conversation.

That was what Finn had said he wanted from the
very beginning. How he had imagined things ending between them. They'd ally for the deal, work on the project, then split amicably and remain friends. But what he

hadn't expected was how much that would hurt. He almost couldn't stand there and get the words out. Because he had fallen in love with her, and as much as he told himself he could be her colleague—

He couldn't. He wanted to be her husband, damn it.

He stopped midsentence and let out a sigh. "I can't do this."

"What?" Jiao had fallen asleep, and Ellie shifted to accommodate the additional weight.

"Stand here and talk about blueprints and city regulations as if there was never anything between us. As if we're practically strangers." Finn bent down, and searched for the woman he knew, but she was hidden behind those damnable sunglasses. "You took the coward's way out, Ellie."

"Me? How did I do that?"

"You didn't file for the annulment. Didn't call a lawyer. You just let us…dissolve."

"Finn, I have a child to raise. I can't be spending my time chasing—" She shook her head and looked away.

"Chasing what?"

She turned back to face him. The noise of the playground dropped away, and the world seemed to close in until it was just them. "Chasing something that will never be." Her voice shook a little. "We pretended really well for a while there, but both of us are too committed to other things to be committed to each other."

"Are you sure about that? Or is that just an excuse because you're just as afraid as I am of screwing this up?" Because he was afraid, scared as hell, to be honest. But the part of Finn that had been awakened by meeting Ellie refused to go away. And kept asking for more.

"I'm…" She let out a breath. "Okay, I am. But that's only because I have so much more at stake here." She nuzzled a kiss into Jiao's ebony hair. It fluttered like down against Ellie's cheek. "I can't take a chance that Jiao will be hurt again. She's already been through so much."

He'd said all this himself, hadn't he? Finn wanted to take the words back, to tell Ellie he was wrong. He understood Ellie's fear, because he'd felt it himself a hundred times before.

Was it fear, or was he trying to push for feelings she would never reciprocate? Was he repeating his past? "If you and I didn't work out—"

"You were right." She shrugged, but the movement was far from nonchalant. "She would be damaged. And I can't do that to her."

"But what about you, Ellie?"

"I'll be fine." But her voice shook again. "I am fine."

"Are you really?" He tried to search her gaze, but couldn't see past the dark lenses. What was going on inside her?

"Of course I'm fine." She cleared her throat, then got to her feet, hoisting Jiao onto her hip to free a hand to stuff their picnic things into the basket underneath.

She was leaving and he hadn't found the magic words to make her stay. "Ellie—"

"You know, Finn, you were right. I was afraid to fall in love. And so were you. It's a risk, maybe the biggest risk of all. But if you don't jump in with both feet, you'll never know what you were missing." She nuzzled her daughter's hair, and he saw the love bloom in Ellie's eyes. Then she bent down and buckled Jiao into the stroller. When she was done, she straightened and faced Finn with an impartial smile. "Anyway, I wanted to thank you for taking over the corporate side of WW. My father speaks highly of you."

"Is that what we're back to? Business only?"

She lifted her gaze to his and this time he could see the shimmer of tears behind her sunglasses. "When did we ever leave that, Finn?" Then she said goodbye to him, and left the park.

CHAPTER FOURTEEN

ELLIE told herself a hundred times that she had done the right thing by letting Finn go. That falling for him would only complicate things. Maybe he was right, maybe she was taking the coward's way out.

Okay, not maybe. Definitely.

She'd done one more cowardly thing after seeing him that day at the park—she'd contacted a lawyer of her own and put the annulment into motion. By now, Finn undoubtedly had received the legal papers from his lawyer. He hadn't called, hadn't stopped by, and her heart broke one last time. He hadn't been serious about them staying together—if he had, he would have fought the annulment. She'd been right not to risk her heart on him.

She dressed Jiao in a bright yellow sundress then strapped her into the stroller and set off down the sidewalk toward the park. The whole way, Jiao let out a steady stream of happy chatter, babbling in a jumbled mix of baby talk, Chinese and English. It was like music to Ellie's ears and she laughed along with her daughter. Jiao had adjusted pretty well to the changes in her life, and Ellie had great hopes for the future. Henry had been spoiling his new granddaughter mercilessly, with clothes and toys and visits.

"You wanna go to the park?" Ellie said, bending down to talk to Jiao.

Her daughter kicked her legs and waved her hands. "Yes, Momma. Yes!" Her English was improving every day. The little girl was bright and was picking up the second language quickly.

"Okay, let's go then." She pushed the stroller and increased her pace a little. "How about today I take you down the slide, and later we can go on the swings and—"

"Gou!" Jiao shouted, bouncing up and down. "Gou, Momma! Gou!"

Ellie's Chinese was minimal at best, and it took her a second to connect Jiao's enthusiastic words with the object of her attention. Across the street, a man was walking a little white poodle. Jiao kept pointing at it and shouting *"Gou!"* Ellie laughed. "That's a dog, honey. Dog."

"Dog," Jiao repeated. "Jiao dog?"

"No," Ellie said softly. "Not Jiao's dog."

"Jiao dog," her daughter repeated, reaching her fingers toward the white pooch, and Ellie pushed forward, putting more distance between them and the poodle. Jiao's voice trailed off in disappointment.

As Ellie walked, her mind went back to the day at the animal shelter with Finn. How he had opened up his heart, and let her see inside for just a little while. Every boy should have his dream, she had said. And so, too, should every girl.

Her dream had been the family in the two-story house. With all the laughter and the Thanksgiving dinners and the messes, and everything that came with that. She loved her daughter, loved her little home in the Back Bay, but a part of her still wondered—

What would it be like to have the kids and the house and the yard and the dog?

Had she made a mistake letting Finn go? Had she let her fears ruin her future happiness?

He had never left her mind, not really, though she had worked hard to forget him. She had come across the concert T-shirt the other day, and put it on, just because it reminded her of Finn. Then after a few minutes, she took it off and tucked it away in the back of her closet. Where she stored all the things that were memories now, not realities.

She'd buy a house in the suburbs and a dog, and have that dream herself. But the thought filled her with sadness.

If she did that, she'd be *content*. Maybe not ever truly happy.

Finn was right. She hadn't been brave enough to really push forward with this relationship when he'd offered her the chance. She'd backed off, so afraid of getting hurt again. She'd preached about risk, and not taken one herself.

She and Jiao rounded the corner and entered the park. Her daughter was practically bounding out of the stroller by the time Ellie stopped and unbuckled her. Jiao dashed over to the toddler-sized play area, complete with a rubber ground cover and a half dozen pint-sized puzzles and mazes for the little ones to play with. Jiao had already made friends at the park, and she toddled off with two other little girls she saw nearly every day. Ellie settled back on a bench and raised her face to the sun.

Something wet nuzzled her leg. Ellie jumped, let out a shriek, then looked down.

At the dark, moist snout of a Golden retriever. "Hey, you. What are you doing here?"

"Looking for you."

Finn's voice jerked Ellie's head up. "Finn." Then she looked down at the dog again, and realized the retriever's leash was in Finn's hand. Her heart leaped at the sight of him and she knew that no piece of paper would ever make that stop. Damn. He still affected her. Maybe he always would. "Is this your dog?"

"Yup. Meet Heidi." Finn chuckled. "Wait. You already did."

She looked down again and realized it was, indeed, the dog from the shelter. "You…you adopted her?"

He nodded. "I did."

"Why? I mean, it's awesome, but I thought…"

"That I was the last person who would take on a dog?" He shrugged. "I am. Or I guess, I was. But something changed me recently."

She still couldn't believe she was seeing the shelter dog with Finn. He had gone back there, and given this puppy a home. It was one of the sweetest things she'd ever seen, and her heart melted all over again. "What changed you?"

He reached into his back pocket and pulled out a piece of paper. When he unfolded it, Ellie recognized it as the annulment agreement. Her heart sank. Had he signed it? Was it over?

"This came to my office the other day, and when I got it, it was like a slap across the face."

"Finn, I'm sorry, but we—"

"Let me finish. It hit me hard because I realized if I signed this, it was all over. I had lost you. Forever."

"You were right, though. I let this drag on, and I shouldn't have. Someone needed to pull the plug."

Finn bent down to her, his face level with hers, those blue eyes she loved so much capturing hers. Her heartbeat tripled, and she caught her breath. "Is this what you really want, Ellie?" His voice was low and quiet.

How she wanted to lie, wanted to just keep up the facade. All along, she'd been telling Finn to take a risk when she'd been the one too scared to do the same. She thought of the future that lay ahead. One where she was content, and never happy, and decided she didn't want that. Not anymore. "No." She shook her head and tears brimmed in her eyes. "I don't."

Finn reached up and cupped her jaw. Ellie leaned into that touch, craving it like oxygen. "Neither do I. Not one damned bit. You were so right about me. I picked Lucy because it was the practical decision, and told myself when it didn't work out, it was because love was too risky. But I was wrong. I never took that risk, Ellie. I never opened my heart. I made up this little list and tried to fit a relationship into a column, and then was surprised when it didn't work out." He ran a thumb along the line of her jaw, and caught her gaze. Held it. "Falling in love is risky. Riskier than anything I've ever done. So I came over here today because I couldn't let the most amazing woman I've ever met walk out of my life. Not without telling her one thing first."

"Tell her what?" It was the only word she could get out. Her breath caught in her throat, held, while she waited for his answer. Damn, this man had her heart. Maybe he always had.

Finn's smile curved across his face, higher on one side than the other, and filling her with a tentative joy. "I love you, Ellie. I fell in love with you the first time I saw you, but I didn't know it. I love the way you talk, I love the way you work, I love the way you smile. Every time I see you, I feel…happy."

Happy. Not content. "Oh, Finn—"

"Let me finish." He let out a long breath, and his gaze softened. "I've never been very good at relationships. Give me a drafting board and a pencil and I can handle anything you throw my way. But when it comes to telling people how I feel...not exactly my strong suit. I guess it was because after my parents died, my little brothers looked to me for comfort. For answers. I couldn't break down and sob on their shoulders. I had to let them sob on mine. And as they got older, I kept on being the rock they stood on."

"They do. I can tell by the way they talk about you. They respect and admire you a lot."

He grinned a little at that, clearly surprised to hear his brothers speak so well of him. "Being a rock came with a price, though. I never wanted to rely on anyone, to be vulnerable to anyone, and most of all, I didn't want to let anyone down. Or take that risk you kept asking me to take." His fingers tangled in her hair and Ellie let out a little sigh. "I told myself I'd keep my heart out of it and then we could walk away and no one would be hurt. But that plan failed."

Across from Ellie, Jiao was standing at the edge of the toddler playground, watching them. Ellie sent her daughter a little wave. "How did your plan fail?"

"My heart got involved the very first day, even if I didn't want to admit it to myself or to you. And still, I wouldn't take that risk." His smile widened. "But then when I got the papers dissolving our marriage, I realized all I want to do is stay married to you, Ellie. Forever. I want to open my heart. I want to jump off that marriage cliff with you and trust that it's all going to work out for the next fifty, hell, hundred years. I want—" his gaze went to Jiao, and the smile grew a little more "—us to be a family. The question is whether you do, too. You took a risk adopting a little girl from halfway around the world. I'm asking you to take a risk and fall in love with me."

She looked into his eyes, and felt the fear that she had clutched so tightly for so long begin to dissolve. Right here was everything she'd ever wanted. All she had to do was reach out and take it. She could tell him no now and watch him walk away.

And regret it forever. She'd been given a second chance. She'd be a fool to throw it away.

So she took a deep breath, then tugged the annulment papers out of his hand and ripped them in two. "I don't want an annulment, Finn. Not now, not later."

She caught the glint of a gold band on his left hand. He'd never taken it off. And her cautious heart finally let go of the last guardrails and trusted. Her husband. The man she loved.

"I don't, either," Finn said then he drew her into his arms and kissed her, a tender, sweet kiss, the kind that would stay in her memory forever. She felt treasured and loved and…like a wife. "I love you, Ellie."

"I love you, too, Finn." She ran a hand through his hair and stared deep into his sky-blue eyes. How she knew those eyes, knew every inch of his face, every line in his brow. "I love you *because* you are the Hawk."

"The man who swoops in and buys up the competition?" He scowled.

She shook her head. "No. That's not what I mean. I looked up hawks one day when I took Jiao to the library. And yes, they're fierce predators, but they're also fiercely loyal and protective. They pick a mate and a nest and they stay there for life." She looked at Finn McKenna and saw the hawk inside of him, a man who would do anything for those he loved—he'd been doing it with his brothers ever since he was a child and he had done it for her simply because she had asked. He was a hawk—a man she could depend upon forever.

"So I should start to like the Hawk nickname, huh?" He grinned.

"Maybe you should." She smiled, then pressed a kiss to his lips. She thought of how close she had come to ending their relationship with a piece of paper. "I was so afraid to believe that you could be the kind of man I could depend on, count on to be there when I needed you. I never realized that the very traits I admired about you were the same ones that make you the perfect man for me. The perfect husband, and perfect father, if you want to be."

His gaze traveled to Jiao, and she saw his features soften as a smile curved across his face. "I want to be the kind of dad who pulls out pictures of my kid's band performance at a meeting and who hangs up their artwork in my office. I don't want to be content, Ellie." He swiveled back to face her. "Not anymore."

"Neither do I, Finn. Neither do I." She held his gaze for a long moment, then put out an arm, and waved over Jiao. "Then let me introduce you to your daughter."

Jiao hurried across the playground to Ellie's side. But when she saw the stranger, she hung back, biting her bottom lip, and giving Finn tentative, shy glances. "Jiao, I want you to meet Finn," Ellie said. "And Heidi the dog."

Jiao wiggled two fingers at Finn, then dropped back a little more. Her head popped up when she noticed the dog. Jiao looked at Ellie with a question in her eyes. "Dog?"

Ellie nodded. "Jiao's dog."

The little girl's eyes widened. She pointed at Heidi, then back at herself. "Jiao dog?"

"Yes," Finn said. He gave the leash a light tug, and

Heidi scrambled to her feet, then pushed her furry head against Jiao's shoulder. The little girl laughed, exuberance bursting on Jiao's face. Heidi licked her face, tail wagging like a flag in the wind.

"Heidi, Jiao dog," the little girl said softly, happily. "Jiao dog!"

Then Jiao paused and took a step back, looking up at the man who was, essentially a stranger to her. "Momma?"

Ellie bent to her daughter's level, and waited until Finn did the same. "This is Finn," she said to Jiao. "He's your dad."

Jiao plopped a thumb into her mouth and hung back, studying Finn from under the veil of her lashes.

Finn put out his hand. "Hello, Jiao. It's nice to meet you."

Jiao paused a long moment, looking up at Ellie, then over at Finn. Her eyes were wide, wondering about this new development in her life. The little girl who had left China with nothing suddenly had a mother, a father, a dog. Ellie nodded. "It's okay," Ellie said.

Still, Jiao hesitated. The thumb wavered in her mouth.

"How about we start with Jiao dog?" Finn asked the little girl. "Would you like that?"

After a moment, Jiao nodded and gave Finn a shy smile. "Okay."

Finn ran his hand over Heidi's neck, and Jiao's smaller hand joined his. The two of them petted the patient dog for a long time, not saying a word, just bonding one second at a time while Heidi panted softly. Then Jiao shifted and stood closer to Finn. She looked up into his face. "Jiao…dad?"

"Yes." Finn nodded then met Ellie's gaze. Tears of joy glimmered in his eyes. "Yes, I'm Jiao's dad. And Ellie's husband."

"You are indeed," Ellie whispered, thanking the stars above for this amazing gift. "For real."

Then Finn reached out both his arms and drew all his girls into one great big hug. And on a sunny playground in the middle of Boston, a family was born. They laughed, and the dog barked, and the sounds of their happiness rang in the air, telling Finn and Ellie that from now on, the floors of their home would never echo again.

* * * * *

COMING NEXT MONTH from Harlequin® Romance

#4327 NANNY FOR THE MILLIONAIRE'S TWINS
First Time Dads!
Susan Meier
Chance Montgomery lays the past to rest with the help of his adorable twin babies and their beautiful nanny, Tory.

#4328 SLOW DANCE WITH THE SHERIFF
The Larkville Legacy
Nikki Logan
Ex-ballerina Ellie leaves Manhattan behind to look for answers in sleepy Larkville, but instead finds dreamy county sheriff, Jed Jackson....

#4329 THE NAVY SEAL'S BRIDE
Heroes Come Home
Soraya Lane
Navy SEAL Tom is struggling with civilian life. Can beautiful teacher Caitlin crack the walls around this soldier's battle-worn heart?

#4330 ALWAYS THE BEST MAN
Fiona Harper
Before their best friends' wedding is over, will ice-cool Damien realize he's the best man for bubbly bridesmaid Zoe?

#4331 HOW THE PLAYBOY GOT SERIOUS
The McKenna Brothers
Shirley Jump
Playboy Riley discovers that it will take more than his blue eyes and easy smile to impress feisty waitress Stace....

#4332 NEW YORK'S FINEST REBEL
Trish Wylie
Sparks fly when fashionista Jo realizes her sworn enemy—the infuriatingly attractive cop, Daniel Brannigan—has moved in next door!

You can find more information on upcoming Harlequin® titles, free excerpts and more at www.Harlequin.com.

HRCNM0712

REQUEST YOUR FREE BOOKS!
2 FREE NOVELS PLUS 2 FREE GIFTS!

✦Harlequin®

Romance

From the Heart, For the Heart

USA TODAY *bestselling author Lynne Graham brings you a brand-new story of passion and drama.*

THE SECRETS SHE CARRIED

"Don't play games with me," she urged, breathing in deeply and slowly, nostrils flaring in dismay at the familiar spicy scent of his designer aftershave.

The smell of him, so achingly familiar, unleashed a tide of memories. But Cristo had not made a commitment to her, had not done anything to make her feel secure and had never once mentioned love or the future. At the end of the day, in spite of all her precautions, he had still walked away untouched while she had been crushed in the process.

The knowledge that she had meant so little to him that he had ditched her to marry another woman still burned like acid inside her.

"Maybe I'm hoping you'll finally come clean," Cristo murmured levelly.

Erin turned her head, smooth brow indented with a frown as she struggled to recall the conversation and get back into it again. "Come clean about what?"

Cristo pulled off the road into a layby before he responded. "I found out what you were up to while you were working for me at the Mobila spa."

Erin twisted her entire body around to look at him, crystalline eyes flaring bright, her rising tension etched in the taut set of her heart-shaped face. "What do you mean... what I was up to?"

Cristo looked at her levelly, ebony dark eyes cool and opaque as frosted glass. "You were stealing from me."

"I am not a thief," Erin repeated doggedly, although an alarm bell had gone off in her head the instant he mentioned the theft and sale of products from the store.

"I have the proof," Cristo retorted crisply. "You can't talk or charm your way out of this, Erin—"

"I'm not interested in charming you. I'm not the same woman I was when we were together," Erin countered curtly, for what he had done to her had toughened her. There was nothing like surviving an unhappy love affair to build self-knowledge and character, she reckoned painfully. He had broken her heart, taught her how fragile she was, left her bitter and humiliated. But she had had to pick herself up again fast once she'd discovered that she was pregnant.

Cristo is going to make Erin pay back what he believes she stole—in whatever way he demands…. But little does he know that Erin's about to drop two very important bombshells!

Pick up a copy of THE SECRETS SHE CARRIED by Lynne Graham, available August 2012 from Harlequin Presents®.

Harlequin® Super Romance®

Enjoy a month of compelling, emotional stories, including a poignant new tale of love lost and found from

Sarah Mayberry

When Angela Bartlett loses her best friend to a rare heart condition, it seems only natural that she step in and help widower and friend Michael Young. The last thing she expects is to find herself falling for him....

Within Reach

Available August 7!

"I loved it. I thought the story was very believable.
The characters were endearing. The author wrote beautifully...
I will be looking for future books by Sarah Mayberry."
—Sherry, Harlequin® Superromance® reader, on *Her Best Friend*

Find more great stories this month from
Harlequin® Superromance® at

www.Harlequin.com

HSRSM71795

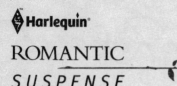

Harlequin®

ROMANTIC
SUSPENSE

CINDY DEES

takes you on a wild journey to find the truth
in her new miniseries

Code X

Aiden McKay is more than just an ordinary man. As part of
an elite secret organization, Aiden was genetically enhanced
to increase his lung capacity and spend extended time under
water. He is a committed soldier, focused and dedicated
to his job. But when Aiden saves impulsive free spirit
Sunny Jordan from drowning she promptly overturns his
entire orderly, solitary world.

As the danger creeps closer, Adien soon realizes Sunny is the
target…but can he save her in time?

Breathless Encounter

Find out this August!

plus
BONUS
STORY
INSIDE!

Look out for a reader-favorite bonus story included in each
Harlequin Romantic Suspense book this August!

www.Harlequin.com

HRS27786